Born in February 1960, third oldest of five children, lifelong Chelsea fan, with a six-year-old German shepherd called Frank, Steve keeps a marine tank, tropical fish tank and has a koi carp pond. He has lived in the same house for 55 years, having bought it with his parents.

I would like to thank my mum for her belief in me and all her support. Love, Steve

Steve Pretlove

PRINCE OLIVER
AND THE
GREEN-STRIPED ZEBRA

AUSTIN MACAULEY PUBLISHERS™

LONDON · CAMBRIDGE · NEW YORK · SHARJAH

A CIP catalogue record for this title is available from the British Library.

ISBN 9781528904025 (Paperback)
ISBN 9781528904032 (E-Book)

www.austinmacauley.com

First Published (2019)
Austin Macauley Publishers Ltd
25 Canada Square
Canary Wharf
London
E14 5LQ

Chapter 1
The Birthday Party

With its severed head spinning across the floor, the suit of armour lay strewn down the hallway; the deafening sound of it crashing onto the stone floor had echoed through the castle. The three princesses and prince knew they were in trouble yet again. This was not the first time they had knocked over one of their parents' prized possessions. They had been playing hide and seek; Oliver, the young prince, had used one of the secret passageways to surprise his sisters; they were hiding behind a green velvet curtain, the suit of armour stood in front of this curtain, so when he quietly crept up behind them and made them jump, well, that's when they bumped up against the suit of armour. They all dashed back into the dimly lit secret passageway that Oliver had used to find them. Sitting in the dark huddled together, they could hear footsteps approach on the stone floor. Good grief, it was one of their nannies who was first to arrive on the scene. "You may as well come out and face your parents," she said. "You cannot stay hidden forever."

Whispering among themselves and holding hands, they decided to come out. They opened the door of the secret passage and stepped out of a giant blue and gold painted vase. "We're sorry," they said.

"Well, you can tell your parents how sorry you are."

Just then, two of the castle servants arrived and started to gather up the pieces of armour. This was not the first time this had happened, and although they were not happy, looking at the remorseful expressions on the faces of the three princesses and young prince, well, they could not stay angry for long, so they continued to pick everything up and start reassembling the armour. The king was not here; he was on a hunt in the forest and would not be back until the afternoon. But the queen was here.

She was in the castle gardens when the accident had occurred; another of the castle servants had been sent into the garden to let Her Majesty know what had happened. Searching the grounds, the servant found Queen Elizabeth down by the lake. The sun was shining and it was pleasantly warm for the time of year. She was painting a picture of two white swans as they gracefully floated across the shimmering water. As he approached, he coughed loudly; this startled the swans who spread their enormous wings and started to run on the surface of the water and took flight. The queen, also startled by the sudden intrusion, had made a sweeping stroke of black paint right across the centre of the painting. The servant approached, "I'm sorry, Your Majesty, for the interruption, but thought you would like to know the prince and princesses have knocked over one of the suits of armour."

"Thank you," she said. "Bring all that back inside, please," she indicated to all the paints and canvases. She walked up the grass bank that took her away from the lake, back towards the castle. She went to find her children. The nanny who had first arrived on the scene had taken them to their chambers. The queen entered the room; her four children sat quietly and nervously, waiting to be told off.

"How many times have we told you to be careful when playing indoors?"

"Sorry, Mummy," said the little girls, and the little prince just smiled. His mother's heart melted in an instant. She loved her children dearly and could not stay angry, and she knew it had been an accident, but once more, she explained why they had to be more careful.

"You could easily get hurt if that suit of armour had fallen on you," she said.

"We promise not to do it again, Mummy."

The king arrived back at the castle after a very successful hunt, dismounted his black horse and passed the reins to one of the guards; the guard led the horse into the stables. "Two wild boars and one stag, not bad for one afternoon," he said to Elizabeth as she came into the courtyard to greet him.

"And I need to tell you that once again, the children have knocked over one of the suits of armour."

"They will hurt themselves one of these days," she said.

Richard just laughed, "Have you any idea how many times I knocked over one of those suits of armour when I was a child?" and he laughed again. He was always jovial and had a way of finding the funny side of everything. Elizabeth sometimes wished he would be more serious; she was concerned for her children's safety.

The three princesses and prince all shared the same birthday. Today was their fifth, 2nd April. The nanny had got them dressed for the party; all three little girls were dressed alike in white dresses that were embroidered with coloured butterflies, and they each wore black shoes and white socks. The prince had on a white shirt and black trousers, white socks and black shoes. They waited for their parents in the bedroom the three princesses shared. It was a huge room with large windows and pink curtains, a fireplace, with a roaring fire lit to keep the room warm in winter; they each had a four-poster bed that was surrounded by pink curtains and had pink pillows on each bed, a room fit for a princess. They also had a rocking horse each, a beautiful dapple grey, with a bright red saddle and reins. There was a large toy box in one corner and a book shelf with lots of books of fairy tales. They loved it when their mother read to them at night before going to sleep. Oliver's room had a connecting door to his sisters; as he was the only boy his room, it was smaller. He had one large window which stood from floor to ceiling and had a heavy blue velvet curtain to help keep out the winter chill; his four-poster bed had blue curtains and blue pillows on the bed. Again, there was a large fireplace which was lit to keep the room warm, for early April could still be extremely cold at night. He had his own rocking horse—it was as black as night, with a brown saddle and reins. He also had a wooden sword and shield, the shield was decorated with the picture of a knight fighting a red dragon, the shield was resting against the rocking horse, and the sword lay on the floor next to it. There was a second door to Oliver's bedroom which opened onto a long hallway that was decorated with the heads of bears, wild boars and a stag with magnificent antlers; he loved to play in the hallway with his sword, fighting the wild beasts on the walls. If he wasn't outside in the castle grounds, then this was the most likely place to find him.

The king and queen entered the room, and in their excitement, the little princesses ran across the room to their parents. With arms opened wide, the king and queen embraced their three daughters with lots of excitement and happy smiling faces. The room was filled with joy, but then the king noticed someone was missing, "Where's Oliver?"

One of the nannies sheepishly stepped forward to face the king and queen, "I'm sorry, Your Majesty, but we don't know where he is, and he was here a moment ago."

The queen was most upset to think that three nannies could not keep an eye on her four children without losing one; the king, on the other hand, once more thought it was quite hilarious, "That's the fourth time in the last ten days Oliver has managed to slip away unnoticed, rather clever I would say. He knows the secret passageways better than I ever did." He laughed. The queen was not amused.

The king called for the guards, "The prince has gone missing; search the castle and the gardens. He must be found."

After a quick search of the castle and the gardens, the little prince was found and brought to his parents. "Oh my goodness," exclaimed the queen, "Where did you find him?"

"Same place as last time, Your Majesty, down by the lake." Once more, King Richard could not stop himself from laughing at the sight of his young son, dripping wet and covered in mud from head to toe; the queen, however, still not amused, gave her husband a disapproving look. He choked as he tried to stop laughing, composed himself and told the oldest and more experienced of the nannies that from this day, she was responsible for the young prince and no one else and if she would please take him away and clean him up. The three little princesses sat with their mother and father while they waited for their brother's return. They were all chattering away excitedly; they knew today was the day they had been waiting for—this was the day of their party.

It was not easy to clean the young prince, full of energy and splashing in the bath; the poor nanny ended up as wet as he was. When she finally got him dried off and dressed, she returned him to his parents. Even the queen was amused to see just how bedraggled the nanny now looked; this time, it was Queen Elizabeth's turn to compose herself. She thanked the nanny, who quickly retreated from the room, muttering to herself, "One of these days, he'll go too far."

The prince, now clean, once more in a white shirt, black trousers and black shoes, joined his sisters and parents. Now they were all here, it was time for presents. "Happy birthday, girls," said Richard and Elizabeth; the three princesses, Alice, Dorothy and Mary each received a china doll with the most delicate hands and feet and most beautiful face ever seen on a china doll; dressed all in white lace, she was truly beautiful. The three princesses cradled the dolls in their arms and were happily playing with them as their parents watched on. "Would you like another present?" asked Elizabeth.

"Yes, please," they answered and each received a bright yellow kite shaped like a butterfly. They wanted to go straight outside to try them out but were told they would have to wait until Oliver had been given his presents. Oliver was the youngest of the four. He had sat patiently waiting his turn, which was quite something for him for he had so much energy, a real bundle of joy.

When they handed him a toy bow and arrows, the queen whispered to her husband, "Are you sure about this?"

"Of course, of course," replied the king. "I was his age when I received my first bow."

The young prince smiled at his parents and gave them both a hug. "Happy birthday, Oliver," they said; the prince just smiled. He was five years old and had never made a sound. Even when he hurt himself and cried, he made no sound, and although he laughed when happy, still no sound. Nobody knew why; even the court physician had never seen anything like it before. All they could do was pray that one day he would learn to speak.

Alice and Dorothy played in their bedroom with their new dolls, accompanied by a nanny; the other two nannies were in the garden with Mary and Oliver. The one helping Mary with her kite was all tangled in the string; she was falling over and thrashing around on the grass like a fish caught in a net. Mary was laughing; the nanny was not. Eventually, she managed to get back to her feet, untangle herself and launch the kite. She was secretly hoping the string would break and that would be an end to the kite. As the kite soared in a cloudless blue sky, the look of joy on Mary's face had the queen in tears of happiness. The king, however, could not take his eyes off Oliver; that poor nanny, he thought, after being soaked by the Prince earlier in the day, she was now being chased by him around the garden with his bow and arrows—she was just able to stay out of reach. The queen, hearing her husband laugh, looked to see what the cause of her husband's amusement was. On seeing what was making him laugh so much, she said to her husband, "I think that poor nanny has had quite enough excitement for one day, don't you?"

He called to his children, and they came to him reluctantly, as they were both having so much fun. "Come, we need to find your sisters, so we can have a party." This put a smile back on their faces; they each took hold of their father's hands as he led them back inside the castle. They followed the queen as she went to find Alice and Dorothy. She entered their bedroom quietly and watched as they happily played together with their dolls; they only realised she was there when she sneezed.

"Come on girls, let's go to the party."

Waiting outside were Mary and Oliver, sitting quietly with one of the nannies. King Richard had gone to check everything was running smoothly. Elizabeth and her four children walked down a long hallway with paintings and tapestries on the walls and a highly decorative ceiling, suits of armour shone silver and gold in the candlelight, carpets covered the floor and all along the hallway, fireplaces were alight to keep out the chill night air. They reached the great hall. The doors were closed. Only when King Richard arrived would the doors be opened; they didn't have to wait long before Richard arrived with a huge smile on his face. "Are we ready?" he asked.

"Yes," shouted the princesses as they jumped up and down with excitement, and so the huge doors to the great hall were opened.

What a wondrous sight assaulted their eyes: hundreds of candles suspended from the ceiling on large chandeliers illuminated the room, a room full of people, from jugglers and jesters to tumblers and musicians, and the biggest banquet they had ever seen. The centre piece was a roasted peacock, with its tail feathers spread in open display, placed on a bed of green leaves; there was also pheasant, wild boar, stag and hare, with an assortment of vegetables from the castle gardens; on a separate table was the centre piece which was a four-layered cake; the bottom three layers were decorated with butterflies, the top layer was decorated with a red dragon, and each layer was filled with fruit. The king made a short speech thanking everyone for making this a special day and hoped they all enjoyed themselves. They ate, and while they were eating, they were entertained by the jugglers and tumblers and jesters, even fire breathers, and when they finished eating, they were dancing as the musicians played. The queen turned to the king, "Thank you for making today so special."

Their neighbours from the kingdom of Elmsdale arrived late; they were announced as they entered the party: King Oswald and Queen Ophelia. They apologised for their late arrival. "We had some trouble with outlaws," they said.

Elizabeth was shocked, "Did anyone get hurt?"

"No, we are all okay," said Ophelia.

"And they didn't get anything; the guards managed to fight them off," said Oswald.

"Where did this happen?" asked Richard.

"It was deep in the forest we pass through, where the bridge crosses the river. We had stopped to let the horses have a drink and they jumped out of the trees above us; it was a complete surprise."

"I will send some of my guards to check it out," said Richard.

"Oh, I wouldn't bother, they are probably long gone by now."

"Nevertheless, I will have them check it out anyway." He called one of his trusted guards over, told him what had happened and gave the order to search that part of the forest. The guard left the room, King Oswald said, "We have a present for each of the princesses and prince, but they had to be left outside. Would you like to see them?"

"I would," said Elizabeth.

"I will show them to you," said Queen Ophelia, and so the two queens left the party, leaving their husbands to enjoy the festivities. Ophelia led Elizabeth into the courtyard, and there before them stood four ponies, three dapple grey and one black as the night.

"We thought it would be a nice idea to match their rocking horses." The grey ponies even had the red saddle and reins, and the black pony had a brown saddle and reins.

"So they really do match the rocking horses the children cherished so much. It's a wonderful idea," said Elizabeth, "I just know they will love them." She stepped forward and stroked each pony in turn. "They are truly beautiful. Come let us go back inside and join the party. I cannot wait to tell Richard." They entered the castle, and as they walked down the hallway that led to the great hall, Ophelia stopped in front of one of the paintings—it depicted a battle scene. There in the centre of the battle was her father, riding a white stallion, sword raised in triumph. They had defeated the invading horde of trolls. Ophelia was Richard's sister, she was remembering the times they had shared as children, their mother had died giving birth to Ophelia, and so they were raised by their father. She remembered how, as soon as they were old enough to ride, he would take them on the hunt. Of course, they would be at the back with two guards, but the thrill of being involved had been exciting. It was eight years since he had passed away and she still missed him. Elizabeth put her hand on Ophelia's arm, which brought her back from her memories. They smiled at each other and continued down the hallway and re-joined the party.

Ophelia went and sat next to Oswald, while Elizabeth took her place by Richard's side. She told her husband of the beautiful gift his sister and her husband had brought. He turned to his sister and said, "Thank you, I cannot wait for them to be old enough to join me on a hunt. I would love for you to join us."

"Of course," she said, "just let me know when and I will be there."

Sitting in one corner of the room was a rather odd-looking old man—short squashed nose, long pointed chin, with beady little eyes, lots of wrinkles covered his face and snow-white hair. He was seated upon a huge pile of cushions, his clothes looked like a patchwork quilt and lying at his feet was a huge white bear; this was no ordinary bear.

"His name is Berwyn," said the old man, "and my name is Percival, and I am a story teller." The children were seated waiting for the story to begin. The story was about a young man who could not speak and who made a long and perilous journey to find the mythical green-striped zebra; for it is said that anyone who can see the green-striped zebra can make one wish and one wish only. This magical zebra lives in a forest surrounded by mountains, there's no way over the top, you will have to go through the caves beneath, but once inside, there are many dangers, dead ends, giant holes and hundreds of tunnels to choose from; choose the wrong one, and you may never make it out. All the while, the young royal children sat captivated by the old man's tale; the king had come over to see what had his four children so enthralled. He listened to the story for a while but interrupted the old man to say, "I am sorry, but it is time for the children to go to bed as it is very late."

Percival asked, "Maybe I can finish my story another time."

The king said he would like to hear the rest of it himself; he offered to put Percival up for the night in a guest bedroom so that he could continue his story the next day. Percival accepted the invitation and said goodnight. A servant showed Percival the way; as soon as the little old man moved from his cushions, Berwyn the giant white bear was at his feet, following his master whom he completely towered over.

Richard returned to his royal guests, told them of the story he had been listening to and how he had invited Percival to stay the night so he could finish his story in the morning. Ophelia said she would be happy to hear the story in the morning, but she was feeling very tired after their long journey. "Of course," said Elizabeth, she asked a servant, "can you show our royal guests to their bedroom?"

The party was now over. The servants were left to tidy up as the king and queen retired to their bedroom—a huge four-poster bed dominated the room, and a fire glowed at the foot of the bed; opposite the door was a large window with heavy velvet curtains, patterned in red and gold, to help keep out the cold night air. "Elizabeth," he said.

"Yes, Richard," she replied.

"Tonight I heard the most fascinating story about a boy who could not speak, just like Oliver."

"Oh, Richard, not again."

"I tell you, Elizabeth, I have a good feeling about this one."

"But Richard, that's what you said about the last one and he turned out to be a scoundrel, just after money."

"But I have already spoken with the fellow. He said he will tell me everything he knows; he does not want anything in return."

Next morning, the story teller did once again tell his tale, but this time to an audience of just five, King Richard and Queen Elizabeth, King Oswald and Queen Ophelia, and without anyone realising he was even there, Prince Oliver. He had used one of the secret passageways and was listening from behind the bookshelf. Berwyn had left Percival's side and had been sniffing at the bookshelf, which nearly gave Oliver away, but he quietly walked back over to Percival and resumed his place at his feet. When Percival had finished, Richard turned to Elizabeth and said, "Well, what do you think?"

Elizabeth looked at her husband and said, "It's a lovely story, what do you think, Ophelia?"

"I agree it's a charming story."

"Ah," Richard said, "but what if it's not just a story."

Elizabeth laughed at him and said, "You're quite mad."

He slumped into a chair. That was obviously not the response he wanted. She went to him and knelt beside his chair and said, "Richard, you're serious."

"Yes," he said, "I could not sleep last night; all I could think about was if there is a chance for our son to speak; I have to seek out this green-striped zebra."

"But Richard, no one has ever seen such an animal; it's just a story."

The king arose from his chair and said, "I have made my mind up, I am going to undertake this journey, and there is nothing you can say that will stop me."

She knew when he was in this mood that that was true. Elizabeth tried to get Oswald to have a word with her husband, "You have been friends a long time; that is exactly why I know there is no point in me saying anything." Elizabeth turned to Ophelia, "Ophelia, he is your brother, surely you can make him see sense."

"I know my brother as do you, and once he has made up his mind about something, there is no changing it."

The king called for his servant, "I intend to make a journey; please make all the necessary arrangements," and he handed the servant a long list of all the things he required, "and I want to leave in four days."

"Your Majesty," said the servant, having looked at the list, "I don't think I can arrange all of this in time."

The king raised his voice and said, "I leave in four days."

"Yes, Your Majesty," said the servant as he bowed and left the room.

Prince Oliver, with a candle in his hand, made his way back along the narrow secret passageway that led to his bedroom. He entered his bedroom via a secret wall panel. After having heard the story told by Percival, Oliver picked up his sword and shield and started to fight imaginary beasts. He played like this until his mother called Oliver and his sisters to join her for some breakfast. Once they had eaten their breakfast, they were taken by their mother to see what King Oswald and Queen Ophelia had brought them for their birthday. They had no idea what to expect, but they were excited. When they stepped out of the castle into the courtyard, they saw four ponies waiting for them, each being held by a castle guard, Oliver sprinted over to the black pony. It had a brown saddle and reins just like the one in his bedroom. He tried to climb onto the saddle, but it was too high; the guard lifted him off the ground and placed him into the saddle and held him tightly in place, so as not to fall. The three princesses followed Oliver's lead. They each ran over to one of the grey ponies. Alice and Dorothy wanted to be picked up like Oliver, but Mary had suddenly stopped short of her pony; it had reared up on its hind legs, and she was scared to get any closer.

Her mother came up behind her and said, "It's all right, the pony was just startled by all the noise and running about; come with me I will look after you." Elizabeth led her daughter by the hand and placed it on the face of the pony. She started to stroke it, "You see it's all right." With that, she put her arms in the air and asked to be put into the saddle. Now all four children were being led around the courtyard on their ponies, around and around they went, circling the stone courtyard. This went on for quite a while, but Oliver was starting to get restless, he wanted to get off, and tried to by himself. Breaking free from the guard's hold, he nearly fell onto the stone courtyard, but his foot was caught in the stirrup and this enabled the guard to catch him before he fell.

Elizabeth decided that was enough for the day. "We can come back again tomorrow," she told her children. Oliver was already off and running into the garden. Her three daughters looked unhappy; they had wanted to ride for longer. "It's all Oliver's fault," said Mary.

"Don't worry," said Elizabeth, "the ponies will still be here tomorrow, and maybe I will let you ride them for longer."

Oliver was down by the lake; he loved playing with the newts and frogs that he found there, but this time of year there were none to be found. He heard a noise, turned around and there was Berwyn, the giant white bear. He towered over Oliver; Percival came along behind Berwyn. "Good morning, young prince," he said, then remembered that Oliver could not speak. But Oliver did smile at the old story teller. He joined Percival on his walk around the lake. This took a good part of the day, and as they walked, Percival told Oliver the rest of the story from the night before, little knowing that Oliver had already heard the whole story, Oliver grew tired on the long walk, for it was a very large lake, so Percival got Berwyn to lie down so he could place Oliver onto his back, and this was how they continued their journey around the lake.

This was the sight that greeted King Richard when he went to look for his son, fast asleep on top of a giant white bear. He chuckled to himself. "I'm sorry we took so long, Your Majesty, I did not realise just how big the lake is."

"That's quite all right, Percival. I hope Oliver didn't cause you any trouble."

"No trouble at all, Your Majesty." Percival got Berwyn to lay down and Richard lifted Oliver from his back and carried his son inside. Percival and Berwyn followed. Richard carried his son down the hallway that had all the heads of animals stuffed and mounted on the walls. He entered Oliver's room and placed him on the bed still fast asleep. Percival and Berwyn went to the guest bedroom they were staying in. Percival was now feeling tired himself and decided to have a lie down before the evening meal; Berwyn lay beside the bed. The evening meal was a quiet affair compared to the night before. At the table sat Richard and Elizabeth, along with Ophelia and Oswald, the four royal children and Percival, with Berwyn laying at his feet; of course, this still meant his head was visible from the other side of the table. King Oswald hadn't had the chance to speak to Percival before and was interested in where Berwyn came from, so Percival explained. "I found him in a cage in a cave with no food or water; he was almost dead when I found him," he said. "He has been my constant companion ever since."

"Fascinating," said Oswald, "I wonder who would have left such an animal to die." The meal was finished, and Percival asked to be excused; he was feeling very tired. Richard said goodnight and Percival left the dining table. Berwyn got to his feet and followed as Oswald watched in amazement. "Such loyalty," he said, and they all agreed Berwyn was an exceptional animal.

The four children, having finished eating, were escorted by their nannies to their bedrooms. The three princesses were helped out of the day clothes and into their night dresses and tucked into their beds. Oliver was far more independent; he entered his bedroom by himself and by the time the nanny had entered his room, he was already in bed with the covers pulled tightly up around his neck. She walked over to the candles that lit his room and blew them out; only the glow of the fire burning in the fireplace provided any light, a soft warm glow, she left the bedroom and quietly closed the door. She walked back through the princesses' bedroom and blew out all the candles; again, just the glow of the fire provided a soft warm light. Oliver waited a short while before getting out of bed. He had been fully clothed the whole time; he was not at all tired. By the glow of the fire, he walked across the room and picked up a candle; he placed the tip of the candle into the fire, so it lit. Now with a candle in his hand, he made his way to the wall panel that opened to reveal a secret passageway. Oliver knew every twist and turn of the passageways and so made his way along the one which would lead him to the garden. Nobody knew, but Oliver loved to visit the garden at night; this was when it came alive with animals you would not see during daylight. He walked across the grass with his candle. The moonlight shone down on the lake, and it looked like a giant sparkling mirror. He had a favourite tree that he loved to climb, and so up he went, just high enough not to disturb the animals below, and he waited. First to appear were a couple of foxes; they came from the dark into the moonlight with their sleek bodies and large bushy tails, sniffing the ground in search of food. Rodents were a particular favourite; they passed on by. An owl began to hoot in the distance, another predator of the night. Then Oliver's favourite put in an appearance: the black and white face of a large badger approached, searching out earthworms, insects and grubs. Oliver sat without moving as he watched from above. Four more appeared, making a family of five; as he watched, the two foxes had returned and came face to face with the badgers. At first, they just looked at each other, then the largest badger raced forward; there was a brief fight and the foxes ran off. Oliver moved slightly, his hand slipped, he lost his balance on the tree, and before he could stop himself, he had fallen to the ground; he landed on his back, with the wind knocked out of him. Oliver lay there for a second before he rolled over to get onto his knees to stand up. Now it was his turn to be face-to-face with the badger; he had dropped the candle when he fell. They stared at each other, almost nose to nose. The badger looked an awful lot bigger being so close. Oliver was so scared of what might happen next, he just couldn't move. Then the other four badgers came to investigate. They all began sniffing around Oliver. He sat still; one licked the back of his hand, its tongue had a rough feel to it, and it tickled, and then suddenly, the largest badger turned away, made a small grunting noise, and the remaining four all turned away and left. Oliver sat still for a while as he watched them disappear into the shadows before slowly standing up. He retrieved his candle and walked back up to the castle, breathing heavily. He felt amazing, he could not believe what had just happened, he felt so alive, and so he made his way along the secret passageway to his bedroom, changed into his bed clothes and climbed into bed. He fell asleep quickly and dreamt of the badgers.

Next morning, Richard was up early; he was going hunting, Oswald had been waiting a short while when Richard came into the courtyard. Today they were going to hunt peregrine falcons. They were accompanied by eight castle guards and the master of the birds; it was his job to look after the birds and make sure they were kept in the best of health. They were to ride out for an hour or so where there was a hill and beyond open countryside. Once there, they could release the birds; to watch the birds flying free high in the sky and then swoop down to take their prey was exciting. The master of the birds would then bring them back by using a lure. So fixated were they on where they were going, no one had noticed a small black pony following behind. Oliver had overheard Richard and Oswald talking of going hunting the day before and so had risen early. He knew exactly which secret passageway to take, and so he was able to get from his bedroom to the stables unseen; he had managed to get his pony saddled and out of his stall and was following them. They were almost out of sight but not quite when suddenly a man appeared in front of Oliver, blocking the pathway. Of course, he could not call for help, and before he knew what was happening, a second man was lifting him from his pony. He was kicking and hitting the man with his small hands and feet—this had no effect—and he was carried off into the forest; his pony had run off down the pathway they had been following. The outlaw carrying Oliver was ducking below fallen trees and weaving his way between bushes of thorns and stinging nettles, and after a while, they arrived at a clearing in the forest where the outlaws had made their camp. As the two men walked into the clearing, another came from a small cottage. "So who have we here then," he asked.

Oliver didn't answer. "We don't know, Cedric; he hasn't said a word since we took him."

"Oh really," said Cedric. "Well, I will get him to talk." He took Oliver by the hand and went over to a fallen tree; he sat down and placed Oliver on his knee. "Now boy, what is your name?"

But Oliver didn't answer. "See, we told you." Cedric did not like it when he felt he was being disobeyed.

"I will soon make him tell me." He placed Oliver on his stomach across the fallen tree. He raised his hand and began to smack him on the back of his legs. Although Oliver wriggled and struggled to break free, not a sound was uttered from his lips.

"Hey, Cedric, that's not normal. Look, the boy's crying but making no sound, maybe he can't talk," said one of the others.

Cedric said, "Tie him up over there; I will decide what to do with him later."

The two kings, Richard and Oswald, were enjoying a great day's hunting; the falcons had put on a truly wonderful display. "The master of the birds has trained them well," said Oswald.

"Yes, I am very happy with them," said Richard. A sound of walking horses' hooves was heard by one of the castle guards; he turned his head and was surprised to see the small black pony with the brown saddle and reins.

"Your Majesty!" he called. He rode up to the pony and took hold of its reins. He started to lead it back to the rest of the party, Richard had turned his horse to see why the guard had called him; he instantly recognised the pony with the brown saddle and reins as Oliver's. "This looks like Oliver's pony, Your Majesty."

"I am sure of it," said Richard. "So where is my son?"

The eight guards started down the hill, following the pathway, calling Oliver's name. As they got to the forest, they spread out. Richard now had hold of Oliver's pony and Oswald was by his side; the master of the birds followed behind. Oliver was tied hand and foot and seated on the ground with his back against a tree, the outlaws were seated around the clearing talking in small groups.

"Shush," one of them said, "I'm sure I heard something." They all stopped talking and listened. There it was again; someone was calling a name. It sounded like Oliver, then again clearer, it was definitely Oliver.

Cedric walked over to Oliver. "Is that your name, boy?" he asked. Oliver nodded. "So we know his name," said Cedric, "but who is he?"

Looking at the clothes he was wearing, he said, "Well he isn't a farmer's lad or a peasant; looks like he belongs to a noble man," and a huge grin spread across Cedric's face. "You know what that means, boys: a big payday for us. Now we need to play this carefully, we need to let them know we have the boy and then decide on a ransom and where to make the exchange."

While this discussion was going on, Oliver was working on the ropes with his teeth. Whoever had tied his hands hadn't done a very good job, and because he had no gag, it was quite easy; all the outlaws were so engrossed in talking about how much money to ask for the ransom and where to make the exchange, no one had seen that Oliver's hands were free and he was now untying his feet. So quickly was he able to untie the loose knots, he was gone before anyone realised.

A ransom had been agreed, and a suitable place for the exchange had been decided. Cedric triumphantly stood up, happy with the decision they had made, and immediately saw Oliver was gone. "Where is the boy?" he shouted. "Where is he, who tied him up?"

At first, no one wanted to own up for fear of incurring Cedric's wrath, they were all whispering among themselves, they knew who amongst them it was, but they did not want to speak up. "So honour among thieves," said Cedric. "Okay, I like that." They all started smiling until he lashed out at the nearest one of the outlaws who just happened to be the biggest one of them all. He caught him square across the face, blood pouring from his nose; he screamed in agony. Fear spread across the faces of the rest of them,

"Now," said Cedric, "who tied the boy?" This time, they spoke up straight away. It was George, and they all pointed in his direction. George didn't know whether to run or plead for mercy, so he decided to run. Cedric picked up a whip that had been lying at his feet; he flicked it once and the air cracked. He flicked it a second time and wrapped it around George's legs. He fell to the floor, unable to free himself as Cedric dragged him across the clearing to where he was standing; now George was pleading for mercy, but Cedric had other ideas. He threw the whip into the air and caught it on the way down. After it had passed over a branch above, he hauled George off the ground and secured the whip so that George was swinging upside down. "Now tell me, how did the boy escape?"

"I don't know, I don't know," screamed George. His head was hanging in line with Cedric's waist. Cedric took out a small knife from his belt; he slowly ran it across George's neck without drawing any blood. George was fearful of what was going to happen next; sweat began to run down his body through the open neck of his shirt, down his neck, it dripped from his chin. Cedric turned away. The voices calling for Oliver sounded almost upon them. Cedric climbed up onto a fallen branch for a better view, he could see the kings' guard approaching. He jumped off the branch. "Leave him," said Cedric, "we need to leave." They picked up their belongings and left George hanging upside down. While all this was going on, Oliver had been observing from above. He had climbed a tree and hidden among the branches. He also had spotted the guards, and now that the outlaws had left, he came down. Unable to call for help, he headed in the direction of the guards. He pushed his way through some brambles and received a few cuts to his hands and face; his feet got tangled in some roots and he fell right in front of one of the guards.

Surprised, the guard shouted, "I have him, I have Oliver, Your Majesty."

All those who had been searching rushed to where the guard was calling. Just as the guard was picking Oliver off the ground, King Richard arrived. He took hold of Oliver in his arms and began crying. "I thought I'd lost you," He looked at Oliver's face and saw the cuts. "Who did this to you?" he asked. Oliver pointed in the direction he had come from; the guards were cutting their way through the brambles, stumbling as they went. When they got to the clearing a few minutes later, they were surprised to see a man hanging from a tree upside down, suspended by a whip. "My God, what happened here?" said Richard.

The outlaw immediately recognised King Richard. Thinking fast, he said, "I found your son, Your Majesty. I was going to return him to you when I was abducted by a group of outlaws; as you can see, they left me hanging when they heard your men calling." Richard had no reason not to believe George so instructed his men to gently lower George to the ground.

Once George was back on his feet, he stumbled. One of the guards caught him before he hit the ground. "Sit here," he said as he led him to a fallen tree.

"Thank you," said George.

Richard was so relieved to have his son back, he gave George his purse. "It's not much," he said, "but it's all I have on me."

George tipped the coins into his palm, there were ten gold pieces, "Your Majesty, this is too much."

"This is a small price to pay for the safe return of my son. Ride with us; we will see you safely to the nearest town."

"Thank you," said George. King Richard sat Oliver on his saddle in front of him, Oswald rode alongside and the guards followed on behind; one of the guards held the reins of Oliver's pony. George was at the back with the master of the birds. He seemed really fascinated by the birds and was asking a lot of questions when in truth he was scared that if he stopped talking, one of the guards might start asking him questions about the outlaws. Up front, King Richard had stopped and called for George. "You should be safe now," said Richard, as he pointed towards a town ahead. "This is where we part company."

"Thank you, Your Majesty." As they parted from the outlaw George said to Oliver, "Now you take care, young man."

As George rode off, Richard spoke to everyone and said, "The queen cannot know about today." Oswald was reluctant to agree at first but in the end, decided it was best.

The third and last day of getting supplies for King Richard's journey was wet and miserable, but thankfully, they had done well and by evening, they had managed to get everything that Richard had requested. The atmosphere in the castle was sombre. Queen Elizabeth would still have preferred for her husband not to undertake this journey, and she had made her feelings quite clear. They were not on speaking terms. Percival was sitting in one of the sitting rooms, telling the royal children another of his stories, with Berwyn lying at his feet. All four children were lying against Berwyn as if he was a giant cushion. This story had a young prince fighting a dragon and so was particularly interesting to Oliver, who stood up and began to fight. The dragon could breathe fire and so was a formidable foe; there was a maiden that needed rescuing, and the prince would be the hero. All four children were totally captivated, and of course, in the end, the prince saved the maiden, and they lived happily ever after. Ophelia and Elizabeth entered the room just as Percival had finished his story. On seeing their mother, the three princesses ran into her open arms; all were talking excitedly at the same time about Percival's story.

"Where is Oliver?" asked Ophelia,

"He was here a moment ago." But once again, he had slipped away through a secret passageway. There was a painting on the wall of a young lady playing the piano, and if you touched the keys of the piano in a certain order, it opened a secret doorway to the left of the picture behind a curtain. Oliver knew exactly where each secret passageway led and after a couple of turns, this one led to the stables. It entered the stables on the top level from what looked like an ordinary wood panel. He checked to see if there was anyone in the stables below before leaving the passageway; it was clear. He climbed down the ladder slowly, so as not to disturb any of the horses. His pony was at the back of the stables with the three dapple greys belonging to his sisters. He walked up to his pony and ran his hand down its neck. He had wanted to go for a ride, but had been told it was too wet. He was bored, so he decided he was going for a ride. He got his small saddle and climbed onto a block of wood. He managed to place the saddle onto the pony's back. With bridle and reins in place, he was set. He slowly walked his pony to the stable door; it really was raining hard. There were some capes for riding in the rain hanging on a hook beside the door; he slipped one of them on. It was meant for a grown-up, which meant he was completely swamped wearing it. He climbed onto a box and then onto his pony. This was particularly difficult because of the length of the cape, but once he was on, he opened the stable door and rode through. Just as they left the stable, there was a crack of thunder and a flash of lightning. The pony, startled, ran at full speed across the courtyard and into the castle grounds. Oliver had never ridden this fast in his life, and the reins were slipping from his small hands. With another crack of thunder and an even brighter flash of lightning, it seemed as if the pony was trying to outrun the storm. Oliver was trying to turn the pony unsuccessfully. On it raced. The rain hitting his face was making it extremely difficult to see anything, as the water ran into his eyes. With blurred vision, he was knocked off the pony by a tree branch that he could not see. He way lying on the ground in the mud and wet with a bump to his head. He passed out.

One of the castle guards had gone to check on the horses because of the storm. He was surprised to see the stable door wide open, and he rushed across the courtyard and into the stables. Pulling the door closed behind him, he secured it shut before checking on the welfare of the horses. At first glance, everything seemed okay. With another loud clap of thunder, a couple of the horses were distressed and reared up, but the guard spoke to them in a soft calm voice, and they settled down. As he moved to the back of the stables, he realised that Prince Oliver's black pony was missing. He raced out of the stables and crossed the courtyard, leaving the stable door wide open once more as he raced into the castle, soaking wet and dripping water everywhere. One of the servants shouted at him, "What are you doing?"

"Where's the king?" he asked. "Quickly!" he said, and she indicated the sitting room on the right; he made his way across the hallway and burst into the room.

Richard and Oswald were playing a game of chess. "What is the matter?" Richard asked, on seeing the guard, who was soaking wet.

"Your Majesty, I have just been to the stables to check on the horses. Prince Oliver's pony is not there."

"What do you mean not there?"

"The pony, its saddle, they are missing."

Richard was out of his seat in a flash; the chess board and pieces were sent flying. "Come with me," said Richard to the guard. They raced through the castle looking for Elizabeth; they checked room after room in their search of the queen. When eventually found, she could see the distress on her husband's face.

"What's wrong?" she asked.

"Have you seen Oliver?"

"He was with us but disappeared when Percival finished his story, why?"

"His pony is missing from the stables; we think he has taken it out for a ride in this storm."

Elizabeth, who had been standing, toppled into a chair as she fainted. "Stay with her, Percival," Richard shouted as he raced from the room. "Sound the alarm."

In the courtyard was a bell. The guard rang the bell. Richard crossed the courtyard and entered the stables. Before Richard had finished saddling his horse, a dozen castle guards had entered the stables. "Oliver's pony is missing," he said. "We can only assume Oliver has taken him out, we must find him."

They all saddled their horses, put on their capes and were off; the rain was still pouring. Richard indicated that half should go one way, and the other half should follow him. The wind had grown stronger; Richard knew this meant that trees were likely to fall. "We must find him." Richard and his men were heading towards the lake while the other men were heading towards the wooded section of the grounds. Oliver's pony was discovered first; it had found a sheltered spot beneath a collection of large oak trees but no sign of Oliver. They started to call his name, but the thunder clap was louder than all their voices put together.

They waited for the thunder to cease and called again, nothing. They were desperate to find the young prince. They knew it was not safe to be here amongst these trees in this strong wind and heavy rain. It seemed as if they were going round and round in circles when suddenly, a hand was spotted beneath a fallen branch; a lump rose in the throat of the guard who had made this discovery. He called to the others as he dismounted his horse. He pushed his way past the fallen branch and there was Oliver, still passed out, blood on his face. Soaking wet, the guard pulled him out from under the branch, lifted him into his arms and walked over to his horse. One of the other guards helped him onto his horse and passed Oliver's limp body up to him. He raced back to the castle in the pouring rain. "Go find King Richard. Tell him I've taken Oliver back to the castle."

The other guards set off for the lake, the strong wind and heavy rain was stinging against their exposed faces. The ground was waterlogged in places which made for slow going, but eventually, they found Richard.

"Oliver has been found and taken back to the castle," said one of the guards, but with the strong wind howling, Richard could not make out what he was saying. The guard realised due to the puzzled expression on Richard's face that he had not heard what he said. Steadying his horse, he rode alongside Richard and repeated, "Oliver has been taken back to the castle." Richard set off for the castle as fast as he could in the terrible conditions. He arrived back at the courtyard and dismounted quickly, leaving his horse standing there as he raced into the castle, calling for his son. A servant greeted him, "Your Majesty, the young prince is with the queen in her sitting room."

He raced on down the hallway and burst into the queen's sitting room; the court physician was already there. "How is he?" asked Richard.

The physician, who had been bent over tending to Oliver, stood up and said, "He was soaking wet and cold. We have dried him off and wrapped him in a blanket for warmth. He has a bump on the head but that is it; he was very lucky."

Elizabeth was kneeling by his side. Richard dropped to his knees beside Elizabeth and his young son. He could not believe he had nearly lost him twice in the last two days. Of course, the queen did not know of the incident from the day before. "Where are the girls?" asked Richard, wiping a tear from his eyes.

"Ophelia took them to bed before Oliver was found." When everyone had left and they were alone, she spoke to him of the journey, hoping this would change his mind and he would not go, but it made him more determined than ever, thinking of the day before. *If Oliver was able to speak, he could call for help.*

He said, "No, I must go." He cradled Oliver in his arms and carried him to his bed. He was fast asleep. The king placed Oliver onto the bed and covered him over, then Richard lay beside his son and fell asleep with his arms wrapped around him for comfort.

Chapter 2
The Journey Begins

The four days had passed. King Richard, ready to leave, was joined by Queen Elizabeth and their children. They had become a travelling party of 14 people, including the king, with ten guards, one cook, a scribe, Percival the story teller, who had agreed to accompany them, and, of course, Berwyn the giant white bear. They left the castle, the king, riding a magnificent white horse, leading the way, with two of the castle guards, one on either side, then came one wagon loaded with provisions driven by the cook, then came a second wagon driven by the scribe with more provisions. Percival had his own little wagon; Berwyn loped alongside his master with ease, the rest of the guards bringing up the rear. The queen watched them go from a balcony, surrounded by her children. They had not a care in the world; how lucky they were, not understanding what was happening. She had not wanted her husband to go, but she understood why he felt the need to. As he reached the tall brick gateway, he turned to wave, and the children waved eagerly in return. The queen waved once and lowered her hand; she turned and took the children back inside. The king watched as they disappeared into the castle. He turned his horse once more and continued through the gate; the queen glanced over her shoulder and watched her husband. A tear trickled down her cheek; she wiped it away with her hand. She hated these times apart. Elizabeth knew there would be dangers, and she would not be happy until he had returned.

Away from the castle, passing through the forest, they came upon an old man on the side of the road. He seemed to be sleeping. Richard stopped his horse and asked one of his guards to check to see if the old man was all right. The guard approached the old man who was lying facing away from him. When the guard leant down and rolled the old man over, he was surprised to find a sword pressed against his stomach. It had happened so fast they were all taken by surprise. Suddenly, they were surrounded by outlaws.

"Well, well, what have we here?" said one of the outlaws. "Why, Your Majesty," he said, as he bowed his head. "I think we will relieve you of your purse, sire." He had drawn his sword and was threatening the king.

"I have no purse on me, you fool, all we have are provisions for a journey."

"Then maybe we should take those instead."

"You cannot have our provisions," said Richard.

"And who is going to stop us?" said the outlaw. All the Kingsguard had been disarmed. Percival and Berwyn had been left behind somewhat, as Berwyn had been drinking at a small stream. No one had even seen them approach. With a silent command from Percival, Berwyn howled a spine-tingling howl and charged at the outlaw who had drawn a sword on Richard. So fast was Berwyn that he knocked the outlaw flying through the air before he could react. As Berwyn turned, he knocked the old man off his feet with his back leg. Two outlaws with swords drawn moved menacingly towards Berwyn. He stood up on his back legs and was at least 12 feet tall, with paws three times the size of a man's hand and with long, sharp-looking claws. He made a swiping motion with one of his paws and sent both men flying across the clearing. They did not get up. The remaining outlaws turned and ran. Berwyn went to give chase but Percival called him back. Richard's guards rounded up the four outlaws, and they tied them together by their hands.

"We will have to take them with us; we can leave them in jail when we reach port. I don't think we will have any more trouble, not now that they have seen Berwyn." It took two days to arrive at the coast where the king's ship was waiting for him, Stephen the young scribe had never seen a real ship before, only in pictures. It was magnificent, over a hundred feet long and thirty feet wide. It had five masts; only one sail was flying as they were tied to the dock. Fully crewed, all the provisions they had brought with them were loaded onto the ship. There was plenty of room for the three wagons and the horses below deck.

The captain greeted His Majesty, "Welcome aboard, we will be able to set sail on the morning tide."

"Excellent," said Richard.

There was a look of surprise on the faces of the sailors when they saw Berwyn. "It's the same wherever we go," Percival said to Stephen. "No one has ever seen anything like him." The outlaws were handed in at the town jail and forgotten.

"I have the charts you requested for this journey, but I must say I have never heard of this island called Colossus."

The king reassured the captain, "I have someone in my party who can help with the directions."

The next day they awoke to a calm sea and light breeze, with a blue sky and fluffy white clouds. Percival was talking to Berwyn; he seemed unhappy about the gentle swaying of the ship. The captain spoke with one of the crew members, "If that giant bear doesn't like this, wait until the open sea." They both laughed.

They set sail and left the docks behind. The smell of the salty sea air was something Stephen had never imagined, and as they moved further away from land, the expanse of open water was quite daunting. Percival joined Stephen as he looked out across the ocean. "Beautiful, isn't it?" said Percival. "I have never seen anything like this before in my life, how far does the water reach, no one knows," said Percival. "I do know that in the past, I have sailed for many a week without seeing any land, but how far it extends, I cannot say."

For two days, it remained calm with fair weather, but on the third day, it all changed; the sky had darkened with huge black storm clouds, the wind had picked up, the sea was rough, and the ship was being tossed about like a toy. Percival had taken Berwyn below. He really didn't like the motion of the sea, being tossed from side to side. The horses were also feeling restless. The guards were doing their best to keep them under control; this was not easy as they were falling over themselves as the ship rocked from side to side.

The captain assured the king, "We will be all right. This is only a small storm; there will be much worse than this."

True to his word, the storm only lasted about two hours, and then the skies cleared once more and everything settled down. The castle guards were all feeling rough, as were Stephen and the cook, but Percival assured King Richard, "I have sailed before many a time. I am quite accustomed to the motion of the sea." Richard had also sailed before and was not upset by the motion although he was not sure how he would cope in a severe storm.

The castle was in turmoil; no one had seen Prince Oliver since King Richard had left. "How is this possible?" the queen screamed. She was beyond despair. Ever since her husband and his party had left, no one had seen the prince. She had sent six guards after the king, but by the time they reached the port, His Majesty had already sailed. She had no idea where Oliver was. If only she had sent the guards straightaway, but what if he wasn't with his father? Still they searched the gardens, hoping he was there, but he wasn't in his favourite place down by the lake. What if he had fallen in? They had no way of knowing. The guards also knew of his love for climbing trees. They had never mentioned this to the queen, and so they had checked all the trees they had found him in before—not a trace of him anywhere. All they could hope for was that he was with his father. Of course, there was always the possibility he had been kidnapped, but no ransom note had been received. The smallest of the castle guards had investigated the secret passageways; Oliver was not in any of them. The three princesses kept asking about their brother. Elizabeth lied and told her daughters that Oliver had gone to stay with King Oswald and Queen Ophelia and would be gone for a while. She hated lying, but it seemed the kindest thing to do. Each day, the three princesses were taken to the stables to see their new ponies; they went with the three nannies who held them as they sat on the ponies' backs, and three guards led the ponies around the courtyard. The little princesses thought this was the best thing in the world, holding onto the reins just as though they were really in control. The queen thought this was a great distraction and so encouraged it wholeheartedly. But nothing could distract the queen from her thoughts. The day before Richard had left, her son had been in an accident, with a bump to the head in the pouring rain, found under a fallen branch. And now this. She was struggling to remain positive but had to for the sake of her daughters. She did not want them to know that Oliver was missing again.

On board the ship, the cook was checking provisions. For the last couple of days, he had this feeling that some of the food was going down rather fast, especially the bread, or was he just imagining this? Berwyn was hanging around the food, yet again, but he couldn't imagine a bear of this size was interested in his bread. Just then, he heard a noise, so had Berwyn. The cook moved the giant bear aside and looked toward the back of the stored food. "Bless my soul," he ran up the stairs onto the deck. "Your Majesty, I think you'd best come and look at this."

Richard followed the cook and said, "What have you found?"

The cook said, "I think you'd better look for yourself." And when Richard looked in the direction the cook had pointed, he found young Prince Oliver fast asleep atop a pile of potatoes.

"How on earth," said Richard.

"Don't know, Your Majesty, small child can get into the smallest of places, and he doesn't make a sound, does he?" His son opened his eyes at the sound of his father's voice and smiled. Although angry at first, Richard smiled at his young son, held out his arms and the young prince stumbled across the potatoes into his father's outstretched arms. Suddenly, it dawned on the King. *The queen, what must she be going through.* She would have no way of knowing that the young prince was safely here with us. But there was nothing that could be done; there was no way he was going to turn back now. He carried his son up on deck and introduced him to the captain and crew, "This is my son, Prince Oliver; he will be joining us on our journey."

"Blimey," said one of the crew members, "who's going to look after him?"

"I will take responsibility for my son," said Richard. Oliver was eager to look around the ship now that he no longer had to hide. There were cabins to explore; he even tried to climb up some rigging to get to the sails. One of the crew members caught him before he managed to get both feet on the rigging and lifted him off.

"You'd be better off staying down here," he said. "Don't want you falling and hurting yourself."

Then Richard took Oliver by the hand, led him to the front of the ship and pointed out at the open sea. In front of the ship and on either side were huge fish; they were leaping out of the water as they raced alongside the king's vessel, Oliver's face was pure happiness, and so the king smiled at his son, but his thoughts went back to his queen and what she must be going through.

Another seven days of fine weather passed without incident, apart from Oliver continually trying to climb up the rigging to get to the sails or go all the way to the crow's nest, but on each occasion, he was caught before he got too far. So he sat with Berwyn, looking out to sea, when something beneath the surface caught his eye. It was very large, swimming alongside the ship, then it disappeared. *Where did it go?* he thought. Oliver leant forward for a better look, hanging over the side of the ship as far as he could reach. There it was again, a quick flash of colour, and it was gone. One of the ship's crew saw Oliver and called out to him to get back, "It's not safe."

Now everyone who had heard the call was looking toward Oliver, just in time to see him disappear over the side. Before Oliver hit the water, he heard the cry, "Man overboard!" As he disappeared under the surface of the water, no audible sound could be heard, only his heart beating in his chest, as he slowly drifted deeper and deeper into the depths. Did he see it? A magnificent creature with blue and yellow scales! Oliver had no idea what this animal was, but for some reason, he was not scared. The creature swam past; looking at Oliver, he circled once. Oliver put out a hand; the creature swam straight towards Oliver and stopped face-to-face. Oliver lifted his hand and touched the blue and yellow face. The animal swam on by; with a large head and a snake like body, it circled once more. Suddenly, the animal turned and swam off. Three crew members had jumped in after Oliver. One had spotted him as he sank deeper towards the ocean floor; he tapped one of the others on the shoulder to let him know he was going after Oliver, and so he swam down. Oliver was losing consciousness. Just as the sailor caught his hand, he started to swim back toward the surface; another crew member swam down and helped with bringing Oliver to the surface. When they broke the surface of the water, there was a small boat that had been lowered from the side of the ship waiting for them. Stephen, Percival and another crew member who had jumped into the sea were waiting in it. The two men in the water pushed Oliver into the air, using one hand each as they clung to the side of the boat. The third crew member pulled Oliver's small body out of the water and into the boat. Richard was in a terrible state, looking down from above. "Is he all right?" he shouted. There was no answer as the two men in the water struggled to get into the small boat. Percival went to work on Oliver; he rolled Oliver onto his back, and he checked to see if Oliver was breathing. He was not. Percival placed his mouth over Oliver's and blew air into his small fragile body. As Percival went to take another breath, Oliver coughed. Out spurt a mouthful of water, and so, Percival rolled him onto his side, water continued to trickle out of his mouth with each cough, but gradually, his breathing got stronger.

Only then did Percival shout out, "He will be all right." Richard sat down with his head in his hands and burst into tears. The small boat was lifted from the surface of the sea. It was raised high enough for the occupants to be helped back onto the ship.

Oliver's small fragile body was carried to Richard's cabin. Percival placed a hand on the shoulder of King Richard. "He will be all right." Richard raised his head and Percival saw the tears streaming down Richard's face. He tried to speak but no words could he say between the sobs. Percival helped Richard stand and they walked to his cabin. Stephen was by Oliver's bedside; his breathing was normal, and he was awake. On seeing Richard, Stephen stepped to one side. Upon seeing his father, Oliver smiled. Still crying, Richard stepped into the cabin and embraced his young son. He kissed him on his forehead and held onto him tightly as if he would never let go again; everyone left them to be alone. The wind was light, so they were barely moving through the water. Suddenly, without warning, a large horse like head broke the surface of the water, followed by a powerful neck. As it rose up above the ship, water rained down onto the crew. One crew member picked up a harpoon but was stopped from throwing it by Percival. The animal looked down upon them. Berwyn stared at the creature in silence and everyone aboard the ship was now looking at this creature from the sea.

"It's a sea serpent," shouted one of the Kingsguard.

"No it isn't," shouted Percival.

"What on earth is that?" asked Stephen.

"It's a seahorse," said Percival.

"A what?" said Stephen.

"It's a seahorse," replied Percival, "quite harmless, but very inquisitive, watch." Percival walked across the deck to face the seahorse and put out his hand. The seahorse lowered its head and Percival ran his hand down the side of the seahorse's face; the scales of yellow and blue sparkled in the sunlight. *Thud!* Something had hit the ship from underneath. The seahorse turned and disappeared at great speed; a dark shadow was seen in pursuit.

"How beautiful was that," said Stephen, "but what is that chasing the seahorse?"

"I don't know," said Percival. "There are many mysterious things in the depth of the ocean."

The next day, it all changed. The weather, having been so calm before, was now like hell on earth. The roar of the thunder was deafening, the lightning seemed brighter than ever, it illuminated the whole night sky, and the gale force winds caused the sea to rise and fall in turbulent waves. The captain was shouting out orders to his crew, "Lower the sails and secure them tightly, we don't want to lose any."

Once again, the ship was tossed around like a toy. Anything that wasn't secure was a possible danger. Below decks the wagons had been tied to try and hold them secure, but the force of the storm was threatening to sink them all. Everyone on board the ship was feeling unwell; only the seasoned sailors were able to cope in these conditions. All through the night the storm raged, the king held the young prince in his arms. After what they had been through yesterday, he could not believe this was happening. Oliver looked into the eyes of his father and showed no signs of fear. Richard tried to smile and wanted to be brave for his son, but his fear had risen inside his body and sat heavily on his chest. Holding Oliver close was comfort for them both. Berwyn was howling, and Percival was trying everything he knew to reassure the giant bear, but nothing worked. This lasted for hours; all they could do was pray they would make it through. Stephen started to pray; he could not believe they would be able to survive such an onslaught. On and on it went. Barrels of food were displaced, harnesses for the horses became loose and were sent flying through the air, horses struggled to stay on their feet, and the guards were trying to hold on to them to keep them safe. Percival had got Berwyn to lay down, but he continued to howl. Up on deck, the crew were struggling to maintain the ship's stability. As the waves battered the ship, water poured from above to the deck below; it was terribly frightening for everyone. Richard cradled his son to his chest and prayed this was not how they were going to die, lost at sea. Slowly, the storm eased, and everything became calm once more. After a night that seemed to last forever, dawn finally broke. Richard left his cabin; Oliver was fast asleep. He went up on deck to find the sailors already assessing the damage. They were exhausted from their efforts of the night.

"How bad is it?" he asked the captain.

"It could have been worse. We got lucky; only one of the sails has got a tear, and we can mend that."

"Any idea where we are, captain?"

"Well, we were blown off course; we should have been able to see land this morning, according to these charts. I will check the charts once more when I have finished assessing the rest of the damage."

"How are the men?" asked Richard.

"A few cuts and bruises, but no one seems to have broken any bones, and more importantly, no one was swept overboard, thank God for that."

A couple of hours later, all the sails were raised; the torn one had been mended, and they were speeding along with a strong wind. Up in the crow's nest, a crew member called, "Land ahoy, I see land." They all looked in the direction he was pointing, and there, before them, was an island. In the distance, it had seemed quite small, but as the approached, they realised this was not the case. But with sheer cliff walls rising up out of the sea there was nowhere to land; they would have to sail around the other side. As they followed the coastline, they were greeted by a vast number of fish that were leaping out of the sea—all bright colours, green, blue and yellow. Stephen was watching the spectacle with Oliver, wondering why they were leaping so high. Soon it became clear: a fish, silver in colour and a lot bigger, was chasing the smaller ones. Leaping out of the water was their way of trying to avoid being eaten.

The smaller fish darted this way and that, to avoid the larger silver fish; sheer numbers helped to confuse it. Then from the depths, a large tentacle reached up and took hold of the large silver fish, grabbed it by the tail and pulled it down.

"What on earth was that?" asked Stephen.

"An octopus," said one of the sailors, and he carried on with his chores.

At last they found a beach and dropped anchor. "I will go ashore with some crew members," said the captain.

"Take six of my guards," said the king. "You never know what you might find."

Having landed safely on the beach, they left the small boat on the sand and went exploring. It seemed perfectly safe, no sign of life, just some noisy birds. They found a pool of fresh water and a variety of fruits. Once they were happy that it was safe, they went back to the ship to report their findings to the king. It was decided they would spend the night on board the ship and all go ashore the next morning. The feeling on board the ship that night was one of relief; they had found land and plenty of fresh water. They went ashore the next morning. The little prince, eager to get out of the boat, jumped into the sea and raced up the sandy beach. One of the guards followed and managed to catch him before he disappeared into the bushes. Everyone else was unloading the supplies when the guard came back with Prince Oliver tucked under his arm. The captain and his crew were left with the ship; they would replenish their supply of fresh water and food for the journey home and wait for the king's return.

Percival and Stephen were walking up the beach together. Berwyn had gone over to Oliver, who had sat down on the sand. As Berwyn got closer to Oliver, the sand he was sitting on started to move. Suddenly, Oliver was high in the air on the back of a giant crab; Berwyn started growling, and every one turned in their direction.

"Oh my God," said Percival as he ran towards Berwyn and the giant crab. The claws on the crab looked easily big enough to snap a man in half. He told Berwyn to back off as the crab was moving in their direction. Oliver had stood up but was finding keeping his balance difficult; the crab lunged forward in jerky movements. Richard and his men had never seen anything like this before; they tried fighting with their swords, but each time they hit the crab's hardened shell, it had no effect.

"How do we fight this?" they asked.

Percival said, "If you can flip it onto its back, it won't be able to get up, but what about Oliver?"

Berwyn had circled around behind the crab as the guards kept its attention at the front. He grabbed one of the crab's rear legs and pulled hard. It momentarily collapsed, and Oliver was thrown onto the sand. Berwyn, quick as a flash, let go of the giant crab's leg and raced to Oliver, picked him up by the foot and carried him away to safety. The oars had been retrieved from the boat they had used to come ashore and Percival was directing the guards, "You need to get in close and push under its belly and turn it over!" This was easier said than done. It proved to be quite nimble for its size, and those claws were massive and had to be avoided. One of the guards got too close and was grasped by the crab in one of its claws; he screamed as the crab tightened its grip. This made the remaining guards fight that much harder, trying to save their friend. It worked! With the onslaught of weapons being used, the crab released the guard from its grip. He fell to the floor in a crumpled heap. Stephen ran forward and managed to pull him out of the way. The fight continued. Richard and two of the guards had gone into the bushes and found some longer pieces of wood. They raced back down the beach; now with two oars and three pieces of longer wood, they were forcing the crab backwards. The sheer size of the crab meant that it was getting tired and with one last effort, they pushed together, forced it up into the air and eventually over onto its back, legs flailing in the air and claws still snapping dangerously, they left it there. "Let's hope we don't run into any more of those," said Stephen.

"There are many things on this island," said Percival, "and I'm afraid much worse than this."

The wagons had a rope attached and were lowered into the sea. They were floated ashore, being pulled by the guards on the beach. The horses swam ashore, and provisions were transported by boat from the ship to shore. The king's party set off on their journey. There was no pathway to follow which made progress through the forest very slow; they had to clear the way for the wagons, hacking at bushes with their swords and lifting fallen branches out of the way. It was hot, thirsty work, but they did not see any other animals for three days. However, at night, the forest came alive, a rustling in the leaves above, a squeal from the bushes, a roar from afar, the sound of something running through the forest, being chased; all these noises kept them alert to the dangers they may yet have to face. They travelled without meeting a single person; all they had for company were the unfamiliar noises of animals. The horses were restless but Berwyn did not seem bothered in the least. On the fourth day, they left the forest behind and were out in the open once again. It was a welcome relief to see the open space of green grass once more. It felt a lot safer than the forest, but the feeling did not last very long as they could see in the distance a black mass weaving its way across the grass flats heading in their direction. They had no idea what was coming, so they just stood and watched as it got closer and closer. Without a warning, from above, a giant bird swooped from high in the sky and grabbed something from the ground; now they knew the black mass was a vast number of animals fleeing from a predator from above, and they were still coming their way.

How could they avoid such an onslaught? Stephen suggested they go back to the forest for shelter. It seemed the only option they had, but Richard had spotted a large fallen tree a short distance away.

"If we can get behind there and pull the wagons in tight, maybe they will run around us." So that was the plan. Still weaving their way across the land, first turning left and then right, it became apparent there was something on the ground that was chasing them as well as from above. The weaving from left to right helped to slow down their progress. Richard and his men were rushing to get everything set as planned; they were behind the tree but hadn't managed to get the horses settled. Berwyn was standing calmly looking over the fallen tree. As the mass of animals approached, Berwyn lifted his head and howled. It was a sound that even Percival had not heard him make before, and as he continued to howl, the approaching animals parted and raced by on either side. The thunderous noise of hooves blocked out everything, the ground trembled, the dust that filled the air made it difficult to breathe, and visibility was poor. It took ages to pass, but suddenly, it was all over. The mass herd of animals had passed by, Berwyn was no longer howling, and as the dust settled and they could see again, there was a large group of predators, one hundred yards or so away. They had captured a large animal and brought it to the ground, one had hold of it by the neck to suffocate it, others were holding it down by its legs, as even more clambered over its fallen body, the animal was still alive and struggling, but not for long. They were all watching from behind the fallen tree, all except Oliver. Richard did not want his young son to witness such a brutal scene. "What do we do now?" asked one of the guards.

"I think we should stay where we are for now, keep an eye on those predators and wait for them to leave before we make a move." And so, they waited; only when the predators had finished eating did they slowly move off, with bellies full; under the midday sun, they entered the forest, in search of shade.

Now they felt it was safe to come out from behind the tree. They mounted their horses, got back on the wagons and started to cross the grass flats that lay before them. Oliver had been put into the wagon being driven by Percival. A guard was sitting with Oliver to keep him safe and Berwyn walked alongside the wagon. In the heat of the midday sun and with no breeze to cool them, it was hard going. The sun was causing a haze to sit a couple of feet above the ground. The heat was rising back into the air as the afternoon wore on and as night time approached, the light began to fade. They stopped to set up camp for the night. They felt vulnerable that night in the open, so they lit a ring of fires surrounding their camp, and although many noises were heard throughout the night, nothing approached. The next morning, as soon as it was light, they were awake. They checked everything before setting off; they each had a crust of bread for breakfast and that was it. The morning air was cool out on the open grass flats. In the distance, they could see a darker line of green on the horizon. "That looks like more trees ahead. That could be a blessing and a curse," said Percival.

"What do you mean?" asked Stephen.

Richard answered, "What Percival means is that once among the trees, we will have shade from the blazing hot sun, but there could be dangerous animals lurking in the forest."

Still, this was the direction that Percival had indicated was the route they had to follow, so on they went. As they got closer, it was apparent that the trees before them were much taller than those they had seen before, and the forest seemed noisier. Colourful birds were sitting way up in the tree tops, singing, and bright orange monkeys were leaping from branch to branch. The guards were alert to every noise as they entered the forest. Berwyn sniffed at the air. A small green lizard ran across their path and up a tree, only to be consumed by a larger lizard that was completely camouflaged by the bark of the tree it was hunting on. A rustling of leaves came from above, then some leaves from above came fluttering down. They looked up into the tree. At first, nothing was visible, but then there was the slightest of movements, and sitting on a branch high up was what appeared to be a small child. They stared at each other in disbelief, then suddenly, without any warning, he leapt from his branch and floated down to the ground in front of the king; only now could they see that this was no child but, in fact, a winged fairy. He introduced himself, "My name is Dante, and who might you be?"

"My name is King Richard and these are my men; we are on an important journey. We have travelled across the ocean by ship. Can you tell me the name of this land?"

"Why, this is the island of Colossus," Dante said, as he bowed graciously and continued, "Your Majesty, welcome to my home."

Dressed in green and with transparent wings, he was almost invisible as he moved amongst the tall ferns. "What an honour this is." With eyes as green as the clothes he wore, he smiled, revealing jagged teeth, which made the smile seem rather sinister.

The king spoke, "The honour is ours, and we hope not to disturb your home as we pass through on our way." They bowed to each other but never losing eye contact, for the king had heard stories about fairies, and something told him that this one was not to be trusted. Dante stood up and smiled again; with the wave of his hand, a table appeared laden with food and wine.

"Please join me for something to eat," As they were all hungry, and not wanting to upset Dante, the king accepted his offer. As they were eating their meal, Dante questioned the king as to where they were going. The young scribe, Stephen, was about to answer, when the king raised his hand, and he stopped; this did not go unnoticed by Dante, who felt the king was avoiding his questions.

Dante asked the king about how he came to own his giant bear. "The bear is not mine," said Richard. "He belongs to Percival."

Turning to Percival, Dante asked, "And how did you come to own such a beast?"

Percival answered, "I do not own Berwyn; he is my companion by choice. I found him caged as a cub and released him. He has been my constant companion ever since."

Intrigued, Dante asked, "Who had caged such an animal?"

Percival replied, "There was no one in the cave where I found Berwyn. He had been left with no food or water and was near death when I found him." Dante just smiled. The rest of the meal they ate in an awkward silence. When finished, the king thanked Dante for an excellent meal and bade him goodnight,

"Goodnight, Your Majesty." Dante's gaze followed the king as he walked away. *What are you hiding from me?* he wondered. The king was glad to get away from the fairy; the questions he asked made the king feel uneasy. He did not trust this fairy and wondered why all the interest in Berwyn.

When morning broke, Dante was nowhere to be seen. Richard was not bothered by that at all until it was pointed out that Prince Oliver was missing. The king was anxious to find his son, ordering his men to search for the young prince. They spread into the forest calling Oliver's name; all morning they searched but found nothing. When they returned they said, "We can find no trace of him, Your Majesty."

Richard was now very angry. "Where is that fairy, and where is my son?" he raged. No one could answer. The surrounding trees were extremely tall. The gnarled trunks made them seem ancient; with exposed roots they looked as though they could move around, and the bushes were very thick. Some had thorns an inch or so long and they were sharp, as some of the guards discovered as they tried to push through them in search of the young prince, but there was no sign of Oliver. The guards told their king they had found no footprints of his son, nothing. Richard's anger was reaching a new level, as was his stress. How could his son just disappear like this, without a trace? They were about to leave and search again when Dante suddenly appeared and holding his hand was Prince Oliver. The king was so relieved, he fell to his knees and opened his arms to hug his young son. "Where did you find him?" he asked Dante.

Dante looked surprised. "I didn't find him," he said. "I took him."

"What do you mean you took him?" roared Richard, his anger resurfacing.

"I took him to see the other fairies."

King Richard could not believe his ears; he was troubled by Dante's behaviour. "How dare you take my son without my permission?" Richard roared.

Dante simply replied, "You were sleeping and the prince was restless. He was not in any danger; he was with me."

King Richard's anger was growing; his face had turned bright red, and the veins in his neck were pulsing. Dante seemed to be enjoying himself. It was fun to him, watching Richard get more and more angry as his face had turned bright red, and so Dante just kept smiling that sinister-looking smile. Richard struggled to control his anger but did not want to upset Dante for no one knew what he was capable of or what he was after. So, not wanting to appear ungracious for his hospitality, but wishing to stay no longer than necessary, Richard took a deep breath to calm himself and thanked the fairy for returning Prince Oliver safely.

He called out to all his men, "The prince has been found; we can be on our way." Everyone returned, Richard thanked Dante once more, they checked they had all their belongings and then left. Dante had wanted them to stay longer, he was interested to learn more about Berwyn, so he was annoyed that they left so abruptly. Dante had disappeared into the forest and once again, he sat watching their every move from high up in the trees, invisible.

With the sun shining brightly on a cloudless day, the air was warm, and the king's party came upon a river. There were some large animals in the water. They were all watching as Richard's party approached. One of the animals made an aggressive gesture by lifting its head and slapping it down on the surface of the water, then it moved swiftly towards the bank. They decided to keep moving. Two more of the animals in the water swiftly moved towards the bank, following them down the river; after a short distance, they turned back and re-joined the rest of the group. Further on, where there were no animals, they stopped to rest and allow the horses and Berwyn to drink. The river was fast flowing and wide; they needed to find a place to cross.

Percival spoke, "Your Majesty, I have been here once before many years ago. I believe I know a place to cross." Percival led the way. His memory served him well; before long, they came across the bridge he remembered. Sitting cross-legged in the middle of the path and blocking their way was Dante.

"Good afternoon, Your Majesty," he bowed.

"Good afternoon, Dante," said King Richard. "How are you?"

"I am well, Your Majesty." He did not enquire how King Richard was, which was rather unsettling.

"May we pass and be on our way?"

Dante, looking at King Richard, said, "I have decided I require payment for the use of my bridge." Aghast, Richard refused. Why, the impudence of the fairy, to demand payment from a king? Dante stood his ground. Richard ordered two of his guards to remove the fairy from the bridge. As they approached closer, he vanished into thin air. Not understanding what had happened and with fear in their eyes, they turned to their king.

"Now what?" they asked.

Dante reappeared and said, "I have a riddle for you. Answer my riddle and I grant you free passage across my bridge, fail and I want one hundred gold pieces."

"And if I refuse," King Richard asked.

Dante instantly disappeared and before anyone realised what was happening, the two guards from the bridge were now in the turbulently flowing river, being swept away, crying out for help.

Dante reappeared once more and said, "You shall not pass."

Infuriated, King Richard sent his men down the river to try and rescue the other two, then said, "Tell us your riddle." Dante's riddle went like this.

"Prince William went to his bathroom, windowless and made of stone. William closed the door; it locked shut. A single candle lit the room. William climbed into his bath, leant forward to turn off the taps, both were broken. Water was covering the floor and rising. How could William keep from drowning and escape?"

King Richard was furious, "That's impossible; there is no escape from such a room."

Dante, gleefully rubbing his hands together, expecting to be 100 gold pieces richer, was very pleased with himself. Just then, the young scribe Stephen stepped forward and said, "Your Majesty, I think I have the solution to this riddle."

"Are you sure, boy?" the king asked. He nodded.

"Go ahead then boy, answer the riddle."

Stephen confidently walked up to Dante, who was watching him approach. Stephen called to Dante, "I have the answer to your riddle."

"Do you now?" Dante said sneeringly. "Let's hear it then."

Stephen replied, "You just need to pull the stopper in the bath to let the water run away."

Dante fell to his knees. "You have outsmarted me this time," he said, "but we will meet again," and then he vanished.

"Well done, boy," said Richard, and just then, the king's men returned; they had managed to rescue the two men from the river. The party nervously crossed the bridge, not sure if Dante had any more tricks waiting for them. King Richard had a firm hold of Oliver; he was determined not to lose him again. Berwyn was at the rear, and so last to cross the bridge, and as he left the bridge, it crumbled into the fast-flowing river. There was no way back now; they would have to find a new crossing when they came home.

Chapter 3
The Gypsies

Four more days passed without further incident in the forest. It was late in the afternoon when they came upon a massive clearing, with a lake in the middle. "This looks like the perfect place to rest for the night," said King Richard.

A fire was lit, and the cook got to work. Having retrieved a bucket of water from the lake, it was placed above the fire and the cook started to prepare vegetables to add to the boiling pot of water; chopped up pieces of wild boar were dropped into the pot, followed by the vegetables—this would make for a good stew. The guards were sitting together, and Richard was teaching his son how to correctly hold his wooden sword which he had brought with him. Percival was feeding Berwyn a great slab of meat from his wagon. He didn't eat meat very often; being omnivorous, he had a wide variety of foods available within the forest. Stephen was sitting, drawing the lake and surrounding forest while they were resting in the clearing. Then the sound of horses' hooves could be heard approaching. Suddenly, a group of gypsies appeared close by. They raced towards the king's party; capes flowing in the wind made them appear to have wings. They came to a halt. Then as they moved closer, the king's guards got to their feet and immediately surrounded the king and his son.

"Well, what have we here," said the leader of the gypsies. There were eight gypsies, all with long dark hair that hung down around their faces; the leader had a long scar on the right-hand side of his face that ran from just below his eye to the very corner of his mouth. Riding wild untamed horses, they approached slowly, ever closer, the Kingsguard drew their swords.

It was the king who spoke, "I am King Richard, what business do you have here, gypsy?"

"Your Majesty, my name is Martinez. I am known as the gypsy king, and this is my clearing. Welcome." They dismounted their horses. Martinez gave the reins of his horse to one of his men and told him to tie them up. The horses were led away and tied up among the trees. Martinez bowed to King Richard, and Richard bowed his head in return. For some strange reason, King Richard was comfortable in the presence of Martinez; he felt no threat from the gypsy king. Richard ordered his men to put away their swords. They seemed reluctant to obey at first, but he assured them it would be all right. The rest of the gypsies climbed down from their horses, whom they led over to the trees and tied them secure for the night.

"We shall have fish tonight," said Martinez, and he and his men set about catching huge fish from the lake; they would eat well for sure. Another fire was lit and everyone was seated around. The fish were cooked, and with the vegetable and boar stew, it was a very satisfying meal. The king talked with Martinez and told him of the journey they had undertaken. He gazed over at his young prince lovingly; he was sword fighting with the youngest of the gypsies. The gypsy king said that he had heard of this place but believed it to be a fantasy.

The king said, "I must explore every avenue to help my son." Martinez understood and nodded in agreement. Two of the gypsies had violins and played in a way the king had never heard before, wild and untamed just like their horses.

The king also told Martinez of the fairy Dante; Martinez nodded. "We have crossed paths with this fairy before, he is not to be trusted." Richard told Martinez of Dante's interest in Berwyn. "He is truly an impressive beast," said Martinez, "how did you capture and tame him?"

Percival, who was sitting beside King Richard, said, "He belongs to no one. He is free to go wherever he wants; he chooses to stay with me simply because I rescued him."

Martinez then said to Richard, "If Dante is showing an interest in Berwyn, there must be a reason. I have no idea what it is, but if he wants Berwyn, he will be back for him."

This worried Richard; he had a bad feeling about Dante from the very first time they had met and had hoped they would never meet again. Martinez asked if Richard would care to join him for a drink of rum. Richard accepted and by the time Richard and

Martinez retired to their beds, everyone else was already asleep. They slept well that night.

When Richard awoke, it was a dark and cloudy morning. The gypsies had prepared some breakfast that they all ate heartily. Martinez said to King Richard, "As we are going the same way, it would be a good idea to travel together. After all, there is safety in numbers." Richard agreed. He asked Martinez about the strange animals they had encountered, "Mostly they leave us alone," said Martinez. "Occasionally, one will come into a camp, but they are usually older and slower and unable to capture live prey; we steer clear of them as much as possible. The giant birds that come from high in the sky are the worst, because they can swoop down so fast, they are upon you before you realise they are even there. In the forest, you need to be alert all the time; you can never be sure of what is lurking amongst the bushes. Sometimes it can be something small that makes for a tasty meal, but you can also become the meal for something much bigger."

Later that day, they met up with more gypsies; they appeared to be not as friendly as Martinez and his men. Amongst them were two female gypsies. One rushed over to Martinez to greet him; the other raced behind and grabbed a handful of hair. They started to fight. The men all stood around cheering.

Richard asked Martinez, "Are you not going to stop this?"

"You must be joking," said Martinez. "To try and come between two gypsy women in the middle of a fight is asking for trouble."

"But they will kill each other," said Richard.

"Don't worry, I won't let it get that far."

The two women were screaming at each other and clawing their faces, kicking and pulling out clumps of hair, then one of the women pulled a knife on the other. Martinez instantly stepped between them. "Enough," he said. They stopped, breathing heavily, and walked away from each other and sat down exhausted. It now felt uncomfortable for King Richard and his men. Oliver was put to bed in one of the wagons as soon as they had finished eating, Percival retired to his wagon, which was right next to Oliver's, and Berwyn lay right outside both. Martinez and Richard were the last two awake once again. Martinez was warning Richard of Dante's greed, he will do anything to get his hands on gold, and Richard was telling

Martinez how he felt uneasy from the very first time he met Dante.

The gypsies were able to accompany Richard's party for the next two days before the road they were travelling along split in two. Martinez and his men were going in the opposite direction to the king; they wished him well on his journey. Martinez said, "I am sure we will meet again someday. Good luck, Your Majesty, and beware of Dante." They turned their horses and rode off into the distance under a thunder of galloping hooves.

Chapter 4
My Name Is Ossirus

Richard and his party had left the forest for open countryside once more. They were ascending a hill covered in grass. Once at the top of the hill, the scenery changed dramatically. The slope descending the other side was nothing but sand, and for as far as the eye could see, there was barely a shrub or blade of grass; it was completely desolate. Richard asked for Percival, who promptly came forward. "What can you tell me of this place?" asked the king.

"Well," said Percival, "my understanding is that this place gets very hot in the day but freezes at night and can take up to a week to cross. That's seven days."

Richard then asked the cook, "Do we have enough provisions for seven days to get across this barren land?"

"Yes, Your Majesty, we do." And so they started to descend. The sand shifted beneath their feet, the wagons had to be driven slowly, they were unstable on the shifting sand, and the horses seemed nervous as their hooves sank deep into the soft sand. Once they had made it to the bottom of the slope, the ground seemed slightly firmer. They began to trek across what seemed an empty place, but it was not as empty as they thought. The sandy ground beneath their feet shifted as they took each step. They had never experienced anything like this before. It was very disturbing at first; it felt as though they were sinking with every step, but they soon got used to the sensation but it was slow going, for the wheels on the wagons sunk deeper than the horses' feet. They travelled early morning following the sun. As it reached its peak in the sky, it was too hot to continue, so they rested and waited until late afternoon to carry on, and before it was too dark, they set up camp for the evening. The nights were indeed cold, but with a large camp fire and blankets for warmth, they survived the freezing night air. This pattern continued for three days with no interruption. There was no sign of life anywhere; even the sky seemed abandoned, with no clouds at all. Their only companion was the bright, blazing sun.

On the morning of the fourth day, however, one of the guards found some footprints, nothing like he had seen before. He called to his king, "Your Majesty, it seems we had a visitor last night." The prints were long and thin, with only what looked like four toes.

"What could have made these markings?" the king asked. No one knew the answer, but they all knew it meant they were not alone after all. Apart from finding the strange footprints, the day followed the same pattern as the previous three. It was the fifth day, and it was the hottest so far, so they rested earlier. While they rested, a vision appeared in the distance. What could it be? They watched as it approached slowly, very tall, very thin, carrying a spear, with long thin feet. This was what had made the footprints. Suddenly, without warning, it sank into the sandy earth and disappeared. Berwyn walked forward and was sniffing the ground where this unknown creature had disappeared without a trace. Percival called Berwyn back.

"What was that?" Richard asked.

"I don't know, Your Majesty."

They were disturbed. No one was sure of what had just happened, but it made them uneasy. Wanting to leave this place as quickly as possible, they gathered their belongings and moved on even deeper into this barren land. That night was very uncomfortable. The horses seemed more restless and the talk around the camp was 'what was that creature' and 'what happened to it'. The next day, the sun was hotter again. As they rested, something stirred, but this time, it seemed to be underground. The earth began to tremble and shake. The young prince clung to his father for reassurance; everybody was looking at each other wondering what on earth was happening when out of the ground popped the tall, thin creature they had seen the day before. Berwyn was the first to respond; he snarled at the strange being, who held up a long thin hand with very long thin fingers. Berwyn calmed and lay down. The king mustered his courage and stepped forward, but the intruder spoke first, with a very deep voice which seemed completely wrong for its appearance.

"Hello," he said.

The king, who was not used to being addressed in such a manner, and by such a strange-looking individual, was momentarily lost for words. When he regained his composure, he replied, "Hello."

"My name is Ossirus, and I live in this desert. May I ask where you are going?"

Richard answered vaguely, not wanting to give the full reason of where they were going to such a strange being.

"I can help you for a price."

"And how big a price is it you require, how many gold pieces?"

"I do not require gold, majesty, but I will take the bear as payment."

Percival stood, "No, you cannot have Berwyn." Richard pointed out to Ossirus that Berwyn was not his to offer for payment, maybe there was something else, maybe a horse.

"I have no need for a horse," said Ossirus. "It is the bear I need."

"Well, you are not getting him," said Percival angrily. Ossirus disappeared as quickly as before into the ground and was gone; everyone was on edge. What is it about Berwyn, first Dante and now Ossirus?

They had almost made it across the desert, for in the distance they could see greenery, trees, at last, and the chance of shade from this relentless sun. Suddenly, without warning, a strong breeze picked up from the left. As they looked, something was moving ever closer and at great speed. At first, no shape could be distinguished. There was sand in the air, so it was almost impossible to keep their eyes open, but as it approached, it was clear to everyone that Ossirus was at the front, followed by a dozen or so creatures of similar height, carrying what looked like a large net. They swept over the travelling party in a dust storm and when it settled, they realised Ossirus had got what he wanted: Berwyn was gone.

How could they move so fast, what did they want with the giant bear, all good questions, but Richard had only one thing on his mind: to get out of this desert as fast as his horse could carry him. Percival was distraught. Berwyn had been his constant companion for many years since the day Percival had rescued

Berwyn; they had never been apart. They finally left the desert. The trees gave much needed shelter from the heat of the sun, so they decided to rest by a small stream. Once again, they were reminded they were not alone. Now back in the forest, all the noises from the animals made everyone even more alert than before. They all drank and filled their water bottles once more. Prince Oliver was playing with his sword, and one of the guards was chasing him when he ran behind a tree and got snapped up by a giant plant. As the guard followed, all he could see was Prince Oliver's feet sticking out from huge pink petals. He swung his sword at the stem of the plant, and the flower's head fell to the floor, opened, and out rolled the Prince, covered in pollen. Another surprise to be wary of: man-eating plants. The guard scooped up the young prince in his arms, returned to His Majesty and explained what had just happened. This was a strange place. They had better be careful; who knew what other strange things existed in this land.

The queen was getting worse with every passing day; she was now refusing not only to eat but also to see her three daughters. Nothing anyone said made a difference; the little princesses were told that their mother was not feeling very well but would be better in a day or two. She sat looking out of the window, wrapped in a blanket against the cold; she would sit without moving for hours at a time. The nannies did their best to keep the little princesses happy. They were so young, they didn't realise what was really going on. They just knew that they missed their brother, father and mother. Elizabeth knew she was not being fair, neglecting her daughters the way she was, but she argued with herself that at least they were being looked after. She could think of nothing else but Oliver and what he might be going through. Not eating and not sleeping was taking its toll on the queen, she could not sleep for she was far too restless, and when she did doze off, the nightmares that followed soon had her awake once more. Even awake, she had begun hallucinating. She was convinced she had seen Oliver down by the lake. She raced from her room at full speed, but when she got there, he was nowhere to be seen. She went into the lake fully clothed and had to be rescued. She was screaming for her son, so convinced that she had seen him there; she was led back to the castle by two guards, one on either side. They were met by the court physician who had heard the screaming. They explained to him what had happened. It was decided that there were to be two guards standing outside the queen's chambers at all times, and at least one person with her constantly; she was not to be left alone, for her own safety.

After what had happened to the young prince, he was not to be allowed out of the wagon alone. Having already encountered a plant that eats children, they wondered what other dangers lurked in the forest. They did not have to wait long for the answer; a rustling sound was heard amongst some bushes in front of them. The guards drew their swords. A group of small deer unlike anything they had seen before appeared. Totally unafraid, they were grazing on the ferns, when suddenly from out of the sky, a great bird appeared, swooped down and carried off one of the deer; the others scattered back into the deep forest. Just like Martinez had warned, the threat from the sky was real. Again, the king and his party were startled; once more they had seen something the like of which they had never encountered before.

Richard asked Stephen, "I hope you're keeping detailed notes, boy."

"Yes, Your Majesty." As they moved through this strange place, there were plenty of noises to keep them on their toes, but they did not see anything, for the bushes were thick and the trees tall. There was water in abundance for drinking but strange-looking footprints lined the river banks. Still, they saw nothing. They had found fruit to eat, but meat rations were getting low; they would have to go hunting. Two of the guards were sent into the forest with bows and arrows while the others had found a small clearing to rest. The two men who had gone hunting, armed with bows and arrows, were quietly moving through the forest. It was thick with large bushes, some covered in extremely long thorns, and the tall trees cast a dark shadow. In places, it seemed more like night than day underneath the tall canopy of branches. A rustling of leaves made them stop. The whole of the forest seemed to have suddenly gone very quiet. They waited, listening for any sound of movement, and there it was: a giant ape with long black hair hanging around its large face and broad neck. It charged on all fours. The terrified guards were rooted to the spot. It stopped a couple of feet short and raised itself up onto two legs; it towered over the guards who were so scared they just couldn't move. They were sweating with fear, and as the sweat ran into their eyes, it stung. Trying not to move was painful. The giant ape had not moved any closer but had started attacking the surrounding bushes in a display of aggression. The two guards, uncertain of what was going to happen, were suddenly surprised when from behind them, a mother ape with its baby clinging on her back appeared. She hurried past the two guards and the large male. Only when she had passed did he cease his display of aggression. His breathing slowed as he calmed, and he fell back to four feet and followed the female into the forest once more. The forest came back to life: birds were singing once more, monkeys were moving amongst the branches overhead, and then their luck changed. Right in front of them, a group of small deer appeared about 30 feet away; they slowly and carefully moved their bow into position and took hold of an arrow. Each fired a single arrow. They both hit their target as the others dispersed back into the forest. They stepped forward and removed their arrow. Picking up the small deer, they then slung them over their shoulder and headed back to the clearing. It hadn't seemed to take very long before the two guards came back, but when they told Richard what had happened, it sent a chill down the spine of everyone present.

"God only knows what we will meet next." The cook started a fire. They would eat well tonight, and one deer would be kept for another day. The smell from the cooking meat seemed to get a lot of attention. The forest was noisier tonight. Something large was moving in the shadows; they could hear its heavy footsteps crashing through the undergrowth, and there was a loud snorting sound. It sounded like a boar when suddenly, a small animal appeared that looked rather like a pig. One of the guards picked up a bow and arrow. He was about to shoot, when crashing through the bushes came what had to be a parent of the smaller animal. It was huge, easily the size of a horse. The guard with the bow and arrow stumbled backwards in surprise, and the huge animal charged forward. It trampled the guard, who had started screaming. The weight of the great beast was too much, the screaming stopped, and as quickly as it appeared, the large animal was gone. Everyone was in shock. It happened so fast. Richard blamed himself. He was beginning to think Elizabeth was right; he should never have gone on this journey and the fact that Prince Oliver was with him only made him feel worse. If his son died, he would never forgive himself.

Chapter 5
The Mountains

The next day, they buried the guard. King Richard said a prayer as they all stood around the grave in silence. Richard, once more, was thinking this journey had not been such a good idea; the dangers they had faced and overcome were only the start. Percival had warned him there would be many dangers, and they hadn't even found the mountains yet. It was dull and grey, with dark storm clouds; the heat from the day before had cooled considerably. The forest animals seemed quieter again today; it seemed they were aware of what was coming. A clap of thunder, a flash of lightning and hail stones like you would never believe, they raced to find some form of shelter. The best place they could find was amongst a group of very large trees. Whether it was the same one as the day before, they could not be certain, but also using the trees for shelter was a large male ape with a group of smaller females. The men and apes looked at each other through the hail storm. The ground was white under a covering of hail, but as quickly as it started, it was over. The giant male ape turned and disappeared into the forest followed by the females.

Richard and his party could not believe what had just happened. "That was amazing," said Stephen.

"They are vegetarian," said Percival. "They would only attack if they felt threatened."

Although the hail storm had stopped, it was still dull and grey and as the day warmed, the humidity level went up. They rested by a stream. Even sitting, they were sweating. It was uncomfortable. A couple of the guards were feeling unwell.

"We will make camp here for the night and carry on in the morning," said Richard. One of the guards who had been feeling unwell was sick in the night. Percival had gone to find some plants that he knew could possibly help the guard to feel better, but he had gone alone. Percival was unaware of being stalked through the forest as he was searching for a number of plants used in medicine. The first time he realised there was a problem was when he was knocked over sideways by a crushing blow. He rolled over and over, and as he rolled, he got glimpses of what had attacked him; it was large and brown. When he had finished rolling and looked back in the direction of where he had come, he saw a large brown bear. He stumbled to his feet as the bear charged forward, baring its teeth and roaring. Percival stood still and raised a hand and the bear stopped in mid-charge without Percival saying a word. The bear then turned and disappeared back into the forest. Stephen, who had followed Percival without him knowing, had seen it all. He now approached Percival.

"What just happened?" he asked. "Why did the bear just stop like that?"

"I have a way with some animals," said Percival. "Right, I have enough plants. I think we should be getting back."

Stephen helped Percival back to camp. He was keen to ask more questions about what he had witnessed, but Percival was not in the mood to talk about it. And so they entered the camp in silence. The guard who had been sick in the night was sweating badly; he had a fever. Percival asked for some water to be boiled. He placed the plants that he had collected into the boiling water and a few minutes later, took the pot of boiling water from the fire. "We just need to let this cool a little." When cool enough, he asked for the guard to be sat upright; he placed a cup into the pot and lifted out some water. "Drink this," he said to the guard, "it should make you feel better."

The guard took a sip and coughed, "It tastes disgusting."

"That doesn't matter," said Percival. "It should help." And so the guard drank. It was difficult to keep down; for each mouthful he swallowed, it felt as though it was coming straight back up. Finally, he had emptied the cup.

"Lay him back down," advised Percival. "It will take a while before it has an effect. I'm afraid we will have to wait at least a day before he can be moved."

"Very well," said Richard. "As we cannot leave, we may as well try and gather more provisions." The cook, Percival and two guards stayed in camp along with Prince Oliver. King Richard and the rest went into the forest searching for anything to eat.

With the sick guard being attended by Percival, the cook was checking provisions, and the two guards were collecting wood to keep the fire going. This meant that Prince Oliver was momentarily unattended, and in that moment, he was off exploring. There was a fallen tree that he climbed onto. As he stood up, he could see a small monkey higher up. The tree was wide enough to stand up on and walk easily but stepping over smaller branches slowed Oliver down. The small monkey moved up the tree easily, but on Oliver went, excited to see the small monkey up close. He had no idea how high he had climbed. Down on the ground, the guards had returned with a heavy load of branches to keep the fire lit.

"Where is Oliver?" they asked.

"I thought he was with you," said Percival.

"No, we went collecting wood for the fire; we thought he was with you."

"But I haven't seen him in quite a while."

The cook heard what was going on and looked out from one of the wagons. "I haven't seen him since I started checking provisions." Now the guards were beginning to panic, "How could we lose him again?"

They started to search the camp and surrounding area of bushes. Nowhere could Oliver be found. Then, from above, a small branch fell to the ground; they looked up and there they could see Oliver. He was hanging from a branch. "Stay there, Oliver," said one of the guards.

"Right, I'm going up," said the other guard. "You wait here in case he falls. You will have to try and catch him."

And so, as Oliver was hanging by his fingertips, one guard started to hurry up the fallen tree, the other waited with bated breath at the bottom. As this scene was unfolding, Richard had a problem all of his own. One of his men had fallen down a hole and had landed on a small ledge, but the ledge was beginning to crumble from under his feet.

Richard shouted to the guard. "Try not to move and we will throw you a rope to pull you out," said Richard. "Quickly, go get a rope from the wagon."

It was Stephen who ran back to the clearing where the wagons were, only to be confronted by everyone looking up into the trees.

"What's going on?" he asked.

It was Percival who replied, "Oliver's got himself stuck up the tree."

"Oh for God's sake," said Stephen. "I need a rope from one of the wagons, one of the guards has fallen down a hole, and we need to pull him out quickly for the ledge he is standing on is unstable. How on earth did Oliver get up there?"

"We were all preoccupied with chores, and no one noticed him missing until it was too late."

"I will have to tell King Richard what is going on."

"Yes, of course," said the guard. He shouted up to the guard in the tree, "Hurry up."

The guard in the tree shouted back, "I'm doing my best." He was only a few feet away from Oliver when something strange happened. The small monkey appeared on the branch beyond Oliver and it approached slowly, cautiously, and then behind the small monkey was a much larger adult monkey. The smaller one moved closer to Oliver, but the larger one made a barking noise. The small one stopped for a second and then crept closer. The guard was on the same branch but on the opposite side of Oliver to the monkeys; he was also edging closer to Oliver. Everyone below was witness to what was happening high above. They all let out a gasp as the guard stumbled on the branch and as it shook, Oliver briefly let go with one hand. The larger monkey had reacted the fastest, he had moved quickly and caught Oliver by the sleeve of his shirt and pulled him up onto the branch. They stared at each other, eye to eye, and then the monkey turned and left. The smaller monkey jumped onto the back of the adult, and they were gone. While this scene was unfolding, no one had noticed the small hand movements made by Percival. No one except Stephen, but he said nothing. The guard grabbed Oliver into an embrace and breathed a sigh of relief. Stephen had finally made it back to Richard with the rope.

"Why did it take you so long?" asked Richard, "Never mind, secure that end around that tree," he ordered. He went to the hole and looked down. The scared guard was terrified as the ledge he was standing on was crumbling away and getting dangerously small.

"Here, grab this," shouted Richard as they dropped the rope into the hole.

"Got it," shouted the guard.

"Right, pull," said Richard. With all of them pulling on the rope, the guard rose quickly back to the surface where he was quickly pulled free from the hole. Now that he was safe, Stephen told Richard what had taken place back at the camp. Without hesitation, Richard was racing through the forest back to camp. He arrived just as the guard was climbing down from the tree with Oliver in his arms. Richard collapsed onto his knees, and the guard placed Oliver on the ground. Oliver ran into his father's arms. Richard was sobbing uncontrollably; he couldn't believe how this had happened. How many more times was his son's life going to be put at risk? He wished he had never started this journey, but now they had come this far, there was no way they could give up and go back home.

Richard carried Oliver to one of the wagons; they watched as he walked past. They all felt helpless and lowered their gaze to the floor; the feeling of guilt was felt by everyone for not looking after Oliver properly and allowing him, once again, to be caught up in a dangerous situation. Whilst searching for food, they had found plenty of fruit. This would have to do for now, for Richard did not want anyone else to go into the forest today.

"Hopefully, tomorrow the sick guard will be well enough to travel, and we can carry on," he said

On waking the next morning, Richard was surprised to see the guard, who had been unwell, was sitting up, eating and looking a lot better. "How are you feeling today?" asked Richard.

"Much better, Your Majesty."

"Do you feel well enough to travel?"

"I believe so, Your Majesty."

Richard turned to Percival and asked, "What do you think, will he be all right?"

"He appears to have made a full recovery, although I doubt he will be strong enough to travel a whole day without getting tired."

"Very well," said Richard. "After we have all had something to eat, we will set off, and when necessary, we will stop and rest."

Once finished eating, the guard who had been unwell was placed in the back of the wagon being driven by Percival, and he had Oliver for company. With the rest of the guards on their horses and Stephen and the cook driving the other wagons, they set off. It was a bumpy ride in the wagon, and even though the guard was feeling a lot better, he soon realised he was not fully recovered. Bouncing around in the back of the wagon, he was once again feeling unwell.

He called to Percival, "Can we please stop for a moment?"

"Of course," said Percival. He called to Richard, who was up front, and told him of his intentions to stop for a rest. A message came back to Percival that the three wagons should stay there and rest. Two guards were to stay with them, while the rest went with Richard to have a look ahead. Richard and the guards travelled for a short while. The forest was beginning to thin out, the trees were not so dense, and the sunlight was penetrating more brightly. As they left the forest behind, the warmth of the sun hit them in the face. It was quite a shock after having been shielded from the heat of the sun by the canopy of leaves provided by the trees.

"I think we've come far enough," said Richard. "We should now return and see if the rest are ready to carry on."

They turned their horses and re-entered the forest. It wasn't long before Richard asked, "Are we going the right way?"

The guard who was leading the way replied, "I was sure this was the right path, but now I am not so sure." The forest looked familiar and yet different at the same time; the tall trees tightly packed together blocking out the sunlight seemed the same, but the bushes looked different.

"I remember bushes with large thorns, but I do not remember any bushes that had flowers," said Richard. He rode over to one of the bushes. It was covered in small, delicate flowers. Only when he leant forward to smell them did he get a surprise, for suddenly, the whole bush became alive with butterflies, and before he knew it, the air was full of them. The tiny, brightly-coloured butterflies had taken flight. What had started out as a beautiful sight suddenly changed. Now that the butterflies were in the air, a swarm of insects descended upon them like a giant black cloud; butterflies were falling to the ground, creating a beautiful covering of bright colours. But this was no longer a scene of beauty; it was an ambush. The butterflies seemed to have no defence against these insects. Only by sheer mass of numbers did some manage to escape and fly off into the distance. Having been distracted by what had just happened, Richard and his men were once more looking around for something familiar. Now with all the butterflies having flown off the bushes, they looked familiar again, so with a carpet of butterflies and insects covering the ground, they continued down the pathway. It wasn't long before they heard Percival's voice as he was telling Oliver a story. On spotting Richard approaching, Percival stopped and asked, "How did you get on?"

"We found our way out of the forest," said Richard. "Are you feeling well enough to carry on?" he asked.

The guard replied, "Yes, I am feeling better."

But Percival said, "I think we need to take it slow and not push too hard."

"Very well," said Richard, "we will take it slow." And so they set forth down the brightly-coloured pathway of dead butterflies that led them into the sunshine once more.

What a relief to be out in the open once more, although this meant they were back in the full glare of the blazing sun and with that came heat. Almost unbearable, strength-sapping heat. Now it was midday, and so they decided to rest again, take on some water and wait for the sun to move beyond the hill they were about to climb. It seemed an age before the hill cast its shadow, as the sun moved lower in the sky; now was the time to climb the hill and see what was waiting for them on the other side. As they made their way up the hill, there were boulders to avoid, easy on horseback, but the wagons had to weave in and out. Still, they eventually made it without any mishaps. From the top of the hill, they were looking down on the biggest forest yet, but beyond the forest, they had their first siting of mountains.

"Let us hope they are the mountains we are searching for," said Richard.

Standing on top of the hill, the wind began to pick up. What started off as a cooling breeze quickly developed into quite a gale. "We had better get down before it gets any worse," said Richard.

The hill going down was steeper than on the other side. The horses could manage with ease, but once again, it was the wagons that were having difficulties. They had to guide the wagons down as if on a twisting pathway; this made it easier to control the speed. Oliver had been removed from the wagon and was riding with his father for safety. The last of the three wagons was being driven by the cook. The left back wheel of his wagon hit a rock—hard, and after all the hard terrain they had previously covered, the wheel shattered. This caused the wagon to fall onto its side. The cook was thrown clear as the wagon continued to crash down the hill. Luckily, it had happened away from the other wagons. As the wagon crumpled and fell apart, pots and pans went flying through the air, food was scattered across the hillside, but one guard was directly in the path of the wagon as it fell apart. His horse reared up onto its hind legs and threw the guard before it ran off. All the guard could do was lie flat on the ground and hope for the best. Everyone watched in stunned silence, for there was nothing anyone could do to help. What was left of the wagon finally came to a halt at the bottom of the hill, and the guard lay motionless. Higher up, they could see the cook making his way down, and one of the guards rode up the hillside to help the cook. Richard had left Oliver with Percival and rode over to the guard lying on the ground; there was no movement. Richard feared the worst. The guard's name was William; he was lying on his front, and so Richard rolled him over. As he did so, William moaned—he was still alive. Richard called for Percival, who left Oliver with one of the guards. On checking the injured guard, Percival discovered that he had a broken leg and some bruising to his upper body. He asked for two pieces of wood and some rope for binding; the wood was placed on either side of the broken leg and tied tightly. William screamed in pain and passed out.

"That should help to hold the bone in place as it heals," said Percival. "But it can take weeks, he will have to travel by wagon." And so, with one wagon lost and another injured guard taking up space in another of the remaining wagons, the provisions they could take with them were drastically reduced.

It seemed like it was one disaster after another, and Richard had had enough for one day. "We will set up camp here for tonight; we will enter the forest tomorrow."

The guard with the broken leg had regained consciousness and was in a lot of pain. Percival had gone looking for some berries to help reduce the pain. He knew exactly what he was looking for; the only problem was they grew high up in the trees and were a favourite of the monkeys that lived there. Percival had been hoping to find some that had fallen to the ground, but no such luck. There were an abundant number of trees that had the right berries, but how to get to them was the question. Percival was too old to climb the tree, and the branches of this particular tree grew very close together, making it difficult for the guards to climb, apart from Oliver. Stephen was the smallest of the group, and so it was decided he would have to climb the tree and retrieve the berries for Percival. The trunk of this particular tree was gnarled and looked very old, but it provided a distorted surface that made climbing easier. The higher Stephen climbed, the more activity there was surrounding him. A small tree lizard ran across the back of his hand as he reached for a branch above his head. The sudden feeling of something running across his hand had frightened Stephen and made him lose his grip; however, when he saw what had run over his hand, he calmed himself and carried on. Percival was watching from below and called up, "Have you found any berries yet?"

"No, not yet," shouted Stephen. He looked down and felt dizzy. He clung to the tree, head spinning, legs feeling shaky; he waited.

"Are you all right up there?" asked Percival.

"Yes, I'm fine," said Stephen.

Taking a deep breath, he moved higher up the tree. Finally, he had spotted some of the yellow berries Percival needed; they were at the end of the branch, out of reach. He sat on the branch and slowly inched his way along but the branch began to bend under his weight; he stopped moving. *Just another foot.* He shuffled forward once more, slowly. Now the branch was really bending as he got closer to the end. Above his head, he could hear lots of movement, but he dared not to look up or down. The berries were still just out of reach; he tried to stretch forward but could only touch them with his fingertips. *Damn, so close.* He needed to get just a little closer. Again, he edged forward slowly, just an inch or so, but it really felt as though the branch would break. He was beginning to sweat, and the fear was building inside himself. He tried taking some deep breaths. The fear was winning, his hands were shaking; he couldn't do this, he told himself. Percival had noticed he wasn't moving again.

He called, "Are you all right?"

Stephen nervously called back, "Yes, I'm almost there."

Percival had heard the nervousness in Stephen's voice and called up, "You can do this." With encouragement from Percival, Stephen reached out his right hand while clinging to the branch with his left. He made it; he had a handful of berries. Percival shouted, "Just let them drop to the ground."

And so, with his right hand, he tugged at the berries and let them fall to the ground. The only problem was, as he tugged at the berries, he lost his balance and fell from the branch he was sitting on. Luckily though, as the branches grew so close together, he was saved from falling to the ground and only fell a couple of feet to the branches below. Cradled in the branches like a giant hand, he breathed a sigh of relief. He was lying on his back facing upwards, and as he looked up, numerous pairs of eyes looked down upon him.

Percival retrieved the berries, and because he was picking them off the ground, he hadn't seen Stephen's fall. As Stephen lay there taking deep breaths, Percival called again, "Hurry up, we haven't got all day." Stephen puffed out his cheeks, took a deep breath and sat up; as he pulled himself up, the animals above dispersed. He climbed from the branch to the trunk once more and found the distorted surface provided perfect hand and foot holds for climbing down; the descent seemed much quicker than the climb up had. Once back on solid ground, he felt much happier. He followed Percival back to camp; the berries were given to the guard to suck. "They will ease the pain," said Percival, and indeed, they did. So, another accident. Each time, they seemed to be getting worse. They would rest here for the night and see how everyone felt in the morning.

The guard with the broken leg had a terrible night; the berries did help a bit but not enough. He had not managed to get any sleep at all; it was a constant throbbing pain that felt like it would never end.

When everyone was awake, Richard broke the news that they would be stuck here for a while, "We cannot expect William to continue with a broken leg." And so they made plans. "Let us see if we can rebuild the wagon." Richard and the guards went to where the crumpled wagon lay. "Let us clear the area, collect what provisions we can use and check the damage."

Two of the wheels had been broken in the fall, one smashed to pieces, but one could be repaired. The body of the wagon was battered but again, could easily be patched up, so all in all, they had been lucky. They just had to build one brand new wheel. Under normal circumstances, it would not be a problem.

"But we have no proper tools for doing the job," said one of the guards.

"We have plenty of time," said Richard.

"We're not going anywhere. We will have to make do with what we have," Percival suggested. "Find me a large enough piece of wood, and I can whittle it into shape with a knife."

And so, using a piece of string held up against an unbroken wheel, they got a measurement; now all they had to do was find a piece of wood large enough. Into the forest they ventured. Percival and the cook stayed with the two guards, William with his broken leg and the other who hadn't fully recovered from his fever. Richard decided to keep Oliver with him and so, with Stephen and the rest of the guards, they went to search in the forest. There were plenty of trees that were the right size; trouble was, they were all still firmly planted in the ground. Now what they needed was to find one that had fallen over. All the time they searched, they were aware of how silent this part of the forest seemed. It was rather unnerving.

"Why does it seem so quiet?" asked Stephen.

Richard replied, "It seems as though all the animals have abandoned this part of the forest."

Then, taken by surprise, they saw a familiar face. "Good morning, Your Majesty." It was Dante, the winged fairy, sitting upon a very large stump.

"Good morning, Dante," said Richard, looking puzzled. "What on earth are you doing here?"

"I told you we would meet again. I see you have run into some trouble; you have a broken wheel."

"How did you know that?" asked Richard.

"I know a lot of things," replied Dante. He then stood up on the stump on which he was seated and said, "I believe this is what you are looking for."

Two guards stepped forward with the piece of string and measured the stump, "He's right, Your Majesty, this is the right size."

"Well, we had better dig it up and get it back to camp."

This, however, was easier said than done. The roots were thick and ran deep into the ground. They used anything they could find to dig the stump out; one guard was using a large stick to scrape away as the surrounding earth that enveloped the tree roots. Suddenly, as he thrust the piece of wood into the ground, he hit something soft. It moved and, before anyone could react, a giant worm had risen from the earth and towered above them and swayed from side to side; at least 10 feet tall and fat—too big to put your arms around. Without warning, it crashed to the ground. Everyone had taken a couple of steps back, but now, it was slowly moving in their direction. They all stepped to the side, hoping it would go straight by, but it turned in their direction once more.

"Damn it," said Richard. He was holding Oliver in his arms. With no visible mouth, they had no idea if this worm was dangerous or not. Then it raised itself in the air again, and this time, one of the guards stepped forward and with his sword, sliced off its head. It crashed back onto the ground, the body writhed, and before their eyes, hundreds of smaller worms poured out of the headless body. One of the guards picked up a couple of the smaller worms, instantly screamed in pain and dropped them to the floor and stamped on them. The larger worm was a dark brown with small red spots, but the smaller ones were bright red.

"I know what they are," said Stephen. "They're fire worms. The adults are poisonous to eat, but the smaller ones are not. But, to avoid being eaten, they are red hot to touch." The guard could testify too, and now they were crawling all over the roots. "If we leave the root until tomorrow, hopefully by then, they will all have gone underground for safety, and then we can come back and carry on digging out the stump."

So, they headed back to camp; at least they had found a stump the right size. As Richard entered the camp, he informed the cook, "We have a guest," They all followed Richard in single file. It was only when the last guard had passed him by did the cook see Dante; a look of annoyance crossed the cook's face briefly, then replaced with a weak smile.

"Good evening," said the cook.

Dante just smiled and nodded as he walked on by. He joined the rest of them around the camp fire and asked, "Where are Percival and Berwyn?"

On hearing his name, Percival stepped down from the wagon where he was attending to William. "I am here," said Percival.

"Hello," said Dante, "how nice to see you again, and where is Berwyn?"

"He is off exploring the forest," lied Percival. He did not want Dante to know that Berwyn had been captured by Ossirus.

Richard asked Dante, "So how did you get here?"

"Like you, I came by sailing boat," he said. Little did they realise that Dante had been travelling with them from the very beginning; his ability to turn himself invisible was most helpful. Stephen was suspicious but waited until he was alone with Percival before airing his suspicions.

"I was thinking the same thing, but why ask about Berwyn? If he was with us at the time, he already knows what happened. Ah," said Percival, "but by asking questions about Berwyn, he is making sure we are not onto him." They sat around the fire and ate what the cook had prepared. Percival went to the wagon with two platefuls of food for William and the other guard.

Dante asked, "What is wrong with them?" Percival told him one has had a fever and is not fully recovered, and the other has a broken leg. "Did you get the yellow berries from the Razeb tree?" asked Dante.

"We got some but not enough," replied Percival.

"They are rather difficult to get to. Not for me," said Dante, and in a flash, he was gone. In no time at all, he was back with a large container full of yellow Razeb berries.

"This should help," he said.

"Thank you," said William. He placed a few in his mouth and sucked on them; the pain in his leg eased slightly.

"When the pain starts to come back, just spit those berries out and replace them with new ones," said Dante. It took a couple of days of digging to remove the stump and get it back to camp. The guard who had the fever was now back to normal. Only William was not able to help with anything, but the pain in his leg had definitely improved. Percival was spending his days whittling away at the wheel; it was slow work with the knife he had to use. Oliver was getting restless being stuck in one place, and on more than one occasion had tried to slip away from the camp. Fortunately, Stephen had been left behind to look after him while Richard and the guards went searching for food; over the next couple of weeks, this was their daily routine. Dante would disappear and the re-appear when it pleased him to do so.

Finally, Percival announced the wheel was finished. To everyone's relief, the guards placed it on the wagon that had been patched up, put one of the horses in place and slowly walked it forward. The wheel worked perfectly. William's leg had not fully healed, but he was no longer in constant pain, and although he could not stand on it, or ride a horse, he could cope with the movement of the wagon. At last, they could enter the forest and continue their journey. They had been able to restock the wagons with plenty of food and fresh water while waiting for the wheel to be finished, so for a week at least, they would be able to travel without having to hunt for food. This meant they could travel each day without stopping, except to eat and set up camp for the night. Deeper into the forest they went, the days seemed to get shorter and shorter. This was because the trees were so dense that they blocked out the early morning sunlight. Only when the sun was directly overhead did it give any real benefit, for as it set in the afternoon, once more the dense trees blocked it out. The moonlight barely seemed to penetrate at all this deep in the forest, and where it did, it cast dancing shadows. As each night, the wind blew; in the darkness, the animal noises seemed more frightening than in the daylight. Oliver would cuddle up to Richard tightly.

They were woken the next day by a crashing sound; something was tearing its way through the forest. They could hear branches snapping and a loud thud as they fell to the ground. "What is that?" asked Stephen as he pointed toward a large animal covered in fur and standing on two legs, leaning on a tree. They watched in silence as the animal moved along the branch, using its weight to bend the branch down so that it could reach the leaves at the tip of the branch.

Percival came and stood next to Stephen. "That's a giant ground sloth," said Percival. "Quite harmless." And he returned to what he was doing, and so they all followed. All except Oliver. Richard hadn't even realised Oliver was there, for he had left him asleep when he came to investigate what was going on. Only now when he went to check on his son did he realise Oliver was no longer asleep. He walked back from the wagon after checking on Oliver and looked around the camp. It suddenly dawned on him...

"Where's Oliver, has anyone seen Oliver?" he shouted.

"No," came the reply, "not since last night."

"Not again," sighed Richard. He started to shout, "Oliver, Oliver, where are you?"

They all joined in, "Oliver," but of course he couldn't answer, and so, without hesitation, they all spread out into the forest calling Oliver's name.

Oliver was approaching the giant ground sloth. He was totally fascinated by the animal, but as he crept closer, he was unaware he was not alone in stalking the great beast. Coming from the opposite direction to Oliver were three large carnivorous cats; slowly and stealthily, they crept forward, closing in.

Snap.

Oliver had stepped on a twig; the cats looked in his direction. After studying him standing still, one of the cats broke away from the other two and started in his direction. Moving cautiously, it crept across the forest floor. Now it was Oliver's turn to spot the large cat; he was standing staring at it, unable to move. When it sprang forward, it felt the cold blade of a sword thrust into its side—Richard had arrived just in time. The cat howled in pain and fell at Oliver's feet, dead. The giant sloth was alerted to the danger as the other two cats sprang forward. Although a vegetarian, it was capable of defending itself; on its front paws, it had six-inch claws which it used to hold onto the branches as it ate. It turned swiftly to face them, and as it did so, it made a swiping movement and caught one of the cats right across the face; it fell to the ground, stunned. The second cat leapt and caught hold of the giant sloth's left arm. It made a horrifying scream and tried to shake it off, but the large cat clung on tightly. The first cat stumbled to its feet, stunned, but prepared to attack again. Just as it leapt into the air, it fell to the ground for a second time, three arrows embedded into its side. Now there was only one large cat left; it was still hanging off of the left arm of the sloth, trying to pull it to the ground. The attack was ferocious but not all one sided; the sloth managed to slash the side of the cat with its right claw, and the cat had momentarily let go. Deep puncture wounds were in the sloth's left arm. The cat attacked again, once more grabbing hold of the left arm. The sloth, using its weight advantage, manoeuvred the cat onto a bush of giant thorns; this was enough to force the cat into letting go and running off. With blood on its left arm from the wounds inflicted by the cat, the sloth also slowly disappeared into the forest. Having witnessed the whole scene, Oliver was in tears. Richard carried him back to the camp and sat with him until he stopped crying; he was cradled in his dad's arms and slowly fell asleep. Once more, Richard was left feeling as though he should never have started this journey.

Next morning, they awoke to the sound of singing birds. It made a welcome change from the deafening silence that sometimes greeted them or the noise of squabbling monkeys racing through the tree tops. They had set off after having some breakfast. William was still riding in the wagon with Oliver, for company; the other guard was now riding his horse. As the day wore on, more and more animal noises were heard; it was as if they were slowly waking up as the sun rose in the sky and warm rays penetrated to the forest floor. Thankfully, the day passed by without any more incidents, and this was the case for the next four days; it was a welcome relief. The next day, the forest trees thinned, and in the distance, they could see mountains. They had made it, but as Percival pointed out, this was only the beginning of their journey. There was still a long way to go to reach the mountains, and so they crossed the clearing before re-entering the forest once more. This part of the forest felt different somehow, although they couldn't quite put their finger on it. Dante had disappeared and not been seen for several days. Richard had been quite happy about that, but once again, he reappeared. "Good morning, Your Majesty," he said.

"Good morning, Dante," replied Richard.

"How are you finding your journey?" asked Dante.

"Tiring," replied Richard, "and you?"

"Oh, I always enjoy travelling to new places and making new discoveries. So where is it you are going?" asked Dante.

"To see an old friend," lied Richard.

Dante knew this was a lie and so didn't bother asking again, "And how's your son?"

"He's doing fine," said Richard.

"There are lots of dangerous animals in this forest, have you come across any?" asked Dante.

"A few," said Richard. "Nothing that we cannot handle."

"Glad to hear it," said Dante, and he disappeared.

Percival commented, "Did you notice how Dante not once asked where Berwyn is?"

"You're right," said Stephen. Richard's dislike for Dante grew after every encounter they had.

Another four days of travelling through the forest without incident and finally, they had arrived at the foot of the mountain. It was unbelievably steep. They could see no way of going over, so now as the story said, they had to find a cave entrance. It was late afternoon; they were at the foot of the mountain, "Clear from trees and bushes, we will set up camp for the night," said Richard. For the first time in ages, it felt quite safe, having a solid wall behind them; at least no animal could approach from behind unseen. However, as they settled down for the night, it began to rain, not particularly heavy, but as they were so close to the mountain, what started out as just a drip soon became quite a torrent of water pouring down on top of them. Now they had to move in the middle of the night; it was difficult to see anything in the dark and the rain had got heavier. They fumbled their way along the face of the mountain and managed to find a dry spot they could all fit into, and so once more settled for the night, only now they were wet and cold. They struggled to light a fire but eventually got one going after some time; the warmth was comforting, and one by one, they fell asleep.

On waking the next day, Richard found Percival standing alone a short distance from the camp, "Good morning," said Richard, as he approached Percival, "how are you feeling this morning?"

"A bit stiff, Your Majesty. This old body of mine is not as fit as it used to be. We got lucky last night," he said as he pointed to the mountain behind them. Richard turned around and looked up; there was a large overhang which had provided them with shelter against the rain. Slowly, one by one, everyone was waking up.

Oliver climbed down from the wagon he had been sleeping in and walked bleary-eyed over to his father who picked him up and said, "Good morning, Oliver," and kissed him on the cheek. For three more days, they moved along the foot of the mountain. At last, they found an opening in the rock face; two guards went inside with torches lit. As the flames of the torches flickered, strange shadows were formed on the cave walls. Only then, with their torches, could they see just how vast this cavernous space really was, with a ceiling so high that it disappeared into the shadows.

They made the decision they would have something to eat as it was midday, and they would continue to look around after having a rest. The cave was big enough for all the wagons and horses to be brought inside. Percival and Stephen were having a look around the large cave when they made a discovery. "Your Majesty, I think you should see this alone," said Stephen. Richard asked one of the guards to look after the prince, and he made his way to where Percival and Stephen were standing. They had discovered a huge pile of bones; some of the bones looked human. There were two skulls that they could make out, but some of the bones were way too big to be a man or woman.

On further inspection, there were bones all over the place smashed against the cave walls; the limbs looked as though they had been ripped off, eaten and tossed away. "Ogres," said Percival.

"What are ogres?" asked Stephen.

"They are about three times the size of a normal man but a lot stronger. They would eat you as soon as they look at you. But I haven't heard of any still alive in years." He then pointed out that all the bones seemed very old. There didn't seem to be any fresh ones at all; indeed, there were no signs of life, only signs of death. The hope they had when they first found the cave was replaced with fear.

"If there are ogres about, and there may be, then we will be in trouble," said the king. But they had no choice; they would press on as planned. Two guards volunteered to search the tunnels. "Very well," said Richard, "but be careful."

So, they lit fires across the entrance to the cave for protection against anything that might show up during the night. In the morning, after a quiet night with no disturbance, they all felt fresh and ready to carry on. There were a lot of tunnels before them, this looked promising, and hopefully, one of these tunnels would take them through the mountains.

It was decided that only two guards at a time would explore a passageway. The two guards set off down the first tunnel; after only fifteen paces, it split into two. They each had a torch and decided to take a tunnel each. The guard who went left found it narrowed soon after the split. He stumbled as the ground sloped downwards and dropped his torch, and as it rolled away before him, it disappeared out of sight into a great black hole which swallowed up the light. In pitch blackness, he had to feel his way along the wall back to where the tunnel had split. As he reached the beginning of his tunnel, the other guard had also returned.

"Mine led to a large hole," said the first guard.

"Mine just ended in a solid wall," said the second.

For the next four days, a similar pattern repeated itself, always with the same ending, no way through. They had marked a cross on the ground at the start of each tunnel they had tried, otherwise it would be difficult to remember which ones they still needed to explore.

"Another day, another tunnel," said one guard to the other.

"Let us hope today is successful."

As they entered into the tunnel, the first thing they noticed different to the other tunnels was the smell; faint at first but the further they ventured down the tunnel, the more pungent it became. The tunnel was wider than any of the others they had already tried; instead of having to walk single file, it was wide enough for them to walk side by side. The smell had got so strong they could taste it, and they started choking. "What the hell is that smell?"

They left the tunnel and stepped into another cave, and then they saw it: lying on the ground asleep, an ogre. They stopped immediately, looked at each other and then started to move back towards the tunnel. A chill ran down their spine as a second ogre to their left had just sat up. They hadn't even noticed it in the shadows, but it had spotted the light from their torches. It sleepily stumbled to its feet, rubbing its eyes. The guards were still moving towards the tunnel. The ogre rubbing his eyes had become alert to his surroundings; he was now fully aware of their presence and roared. Before they knew it, five more ogres roused from their sleep. They had no choice but to run. They had reached the tunnel just as an ogre coming from the side put out a giant hand and tried to grab them. He roared in frustration; now they were racing through the tunnel, with the ogres close behind. The terrifying noise they were making had been heard back at King Richard's camp as it echoed through the tunnel.

"What is that?" asked Stephen; he looked across at Percival and then King Richard.

"Ogres," was the reply.

The two guards were struggling to stay ahead. The ogres had a much larger stride and were gaining, but they were fighting amongst themselves in pursuit of the guards. This handed the advantage back to them, and as the tunnel twisted and turned, it was easier for the guards to manoeuvre.

Still the chase was on, and the roar of the ogres grew louder. One guard stumbled and fell; the other stopped to help him back to his feet. Just as they were getting up, a large hand reached forward from the shadow and grabbed an ankle, but Richard and his guards had arrived just in time. The ogre began to lift the guard into the air by his foot but was met with an onslaught of arrows to his arm; he instantly dropped the guard and pulled his arm back, howling in pain. Another ogre pushed his way past the first and came face to face with Richard and his men. He roared at them as he hit his fist into the ground. The earth shook; they stumbled but did not fall. They fired another set of arrows, this time hitting the ogre full in the face. He howled but did not retreat. He lunged forward, and they all stepped backwards. The tunnel behind them was narrower.

"Quickly," shouted Percival, "the ogre will not fit through here." And so they all filed back down the tunnel. Percival was right; the ogre was too big to follow. Just when they thought they were safe, a long arm and large hand appeared, feeling the ground, searching. One of the guards stuck a sword into the back of its hand, and the ogre pulled its arm back, roaring in pain once more. They moved away from the tunnel, back into the cave itself. At least they were safe for now, but the question now was: do the ogres know how to get into this cave? No one knew the answer, so a decision had to be made. There were more tunnels they could search, but this could lead them, once again, into contact with the ogres; but what choice did they have really? They needed to find a way through the mountain. But not today, now they needed to rest. Fires were lit at the entrance of the cave for safety overnight. The ogres could still be heard in the tunnel as they roared in defiance, and the echo carried through the tunnel. Eventually, it went quiet as the night wore on. Next day, the decision was made. They would try another tunnel, but this time, they would be very careful; they didn't want a repeat of yesterday. Once more, two guards set off down a yet unexplored tunnel, but sitting around, waiting for them to come back with news was boring. Dead boring. Percival and Stephen had stepped outside, Richard was off with the guards collecting more fresh water and fruit, and Oliver had been left with the cook. After a few minutes of fresh air, Percival and Stephen stepped back into the cave.

"Where's Oliver?" asked Stephen.

"He's just there," said the cook, pointing in the direction of the fire.

"Where?" said Stephen.

"Well, he was right there just a second ago; he can't have gone far." And so they started calling his name. Now Oliver, being Oliver, heard them calling his name, but he was on a mission and was not about to turn back; he wanted to see the ogres for himself. He slowly made his way along the tunnel from the day before. Torch in hand, he moved cautiously, listening intently. He could hear breathing; it was slow and constant. They were sleeping. The strong pungent smell had hit him like a smack in the face; he coughed but no sound, so no one stirred. He ventured further amongst them to get a closer look. He got so close to one ogre's face that when it exhaled a deep breath, it knocked Oliver off his feet. Just as he stood up, another ogre rolled over, and as his arm fell to the ground, it just narrowly missed hitting Oliver.

Percival, Stephen and the cook had also made their way down the tunnel. They could see Oliver walking amongst the ogres, and they beckoned for him to come to them. He shook his head.

"For God's sake," whispered Stephen; he would have to get Oliver and bring him back. He sent Percival and the cook back to find Richard. He may need help, so they left Stephen trying to entice Oliver to come to him. Just as Stephen went to step clear of the tunnel, one of the ogres sat up. Stephen was watching

Oliver, as well as keeping an eye on the ogre. Oliver had seen the ogre sit up also. He was now scared, but there were three ogres between himself and Stephen, and he didn't know what to do. Stephen was looking for a way to get to Oliver. There were some boulders to his right. If he could reach those, he might be able to hide behind them and make his way to Oliver. But before he made up his mind, Oliver ran straight past all three ogres, including the one that was sitting up and dropped his torch on the ground as he reached Stephen. He had been spotted, for the ogre was on his feet and roared. The other ogres awakened as the first one entered the tunnel, and they were in pursuit. Stephen had picked Oliver up and was running with him in his arms, which made it difficult to run; they were being caught up with, and they were a long way from safety. Stephen had spotted a split in the tunnel wall on his way through and was now hoping to find it again on his way back, for he didn't think he could outrun the ogres.

"There it is!" He pushed Oliver inside and squeezed in behind, but it only went back about four feet. The ogre had seen them enter and was at the entrance of the split. He dropped to his knees and placed his hands on the ground to support his body and leant forward to place one eye against the opening. Stephen thrust the torch into the ogre's eye. He recoiled in pain, screaming. A second ogre climbed over the first; now he was at the entrance. Again, he had to get down on all fours, but this time, he placed a giant hand into the hole. He was making grabbing movements with his hand, but it was so fat he just couldn't squeeze his arm in far enough to reach. He roared with frustration and withdrew his hand. Stephen and Oliver were trapped, and there was only one way out.

The ogres seemed to be talking to each other, but Stephen could not understand what they were saying and so they sat and waited. It wasn't long before something was being pushed into where Stephen and Oliver were trapped. It was a piece of broken bone. Oliver and Stephen had to somehow avoid this weapon, as it was thrust into their space, withdrawn and thrust in, again and again. Stephen dropped the torch, and as he did so, it showed a gap at the bottom of the wall to their left. He pushed Oliver into the gap, and the young prince disappeared. Stephen followed, grabbing the torch from the ground as he went. They had fallen into a different cave, and although they only had one torch, it was bright inside this cave for there was something on the walls that was reflecting the light. There was no smell in this cave and no visible sign of ogres. For now, it seemed they were safe, but how would they find their way back to the others?

Meanwhile, Percival and the cook had returned to the main cave; Richard and his men arrived back at the same time, Percival was panting heavily as he approached King Richard. Richard noticed this and became worried.

"Where is Oliver?" he asked. Still panting, Percival explained what had happened. Richard was in shock; once more Oliver had got himself in trouble. "Can no one be trusted to keep an eye on him?" he raged.

He grabbed a torch and lit it from the fire. He raced into the tunnel, followed by the guards, some carrying torches, but all carrying either a sword or bow. As they moved along the tunnel, they could hear the ogres. They stopped running and started to walk slowly towards the sound being made by the ogres. They knew they were close, so they stopped. Richard had raised a hand; he crept forward with his torch. He could hear a tapping noise, but he didn't know what it meant, so he moved closer. Then he spotted it: an ogre lying on its side with its hand pushed into a hole in the wall. As he watched, he observed the ogre push a broken bone into the hole and then withdraw it; he repeated this over and over again. *So that's where Oliver must be*, he thought. He returned to his men and told them what he had seen, "Right, how do we drive them off?" he said. One guard suggested they all charge together and drive them away with their swords. Richard didn't think that would work. "Any more ideas?" he asked.

"How about trying to drive them back with fire?" said William.

Richard liked this idea, "But how do we execute it?"

"Make way, make way," it was Percival. He was carrying a blanket in his arms which he dropped at Richard's feet.

"What's this?" Richard asked. He bent down to retrieve what Percival had brought wrapped in the blanket.

"They are seed pods from the Atapat tree. Watch this," he took the one Richard was holding. The seed pods were covered in what looked like hair. As Percival placed it against the torch, the hair caught fire, then he threw it at the ogres. It exploded on impact against the rocks; the ogres were startled and stopped what they were doing.

"Quickly," said Percival. Richard threw another; once more, it exploded on impact. The ogres had no idea what was happening, but they didn't seem to like it, so Richard continued to throw them all, one after the other. Eventually, the ogres were driven off. Richard ran forward, disappeared into the split and found the bone fragment lying on the ground but no sign of Oliver or Stephen,

"Well, where are they?" he said.

"I'm sorry, Your Majesty, I don't know," said Percival. "I had assumed, the same as you, that they were trapped inside by the ogres."

Oliver and Stephen were looking around the cave they had entered by mistake. They had dropped through a hole and it was too high to reach so they couldn't go back that way. Stephen tried calling for help, no answer. He had a firm hold of Oliver's hand; he didn't want him running off again. There were quite a few tunnels leading off from this cave, but Stephen just was not sure of the best thing to do. He decided to wait. After Richard had come back out of the split in the rock, Percival had entered. With a torch in hand, he searched the wall for any more splits they could have gone through—nothing. He looked up to see if they had managed to climb out, but there was no way they could have climbed out. *There must be a way out,* thought Percival, then he had the idea. *If they didn't go up, they must have gone down.* He lowered the torch to the floor and slowly circled his way around; there it was: the gap beneath the rock. He called Richard, who entered the split and found Percival on his hands and knees.

"What are you doing down there?" he asked.

"I think I've found how Oliver and Stephen got out."

Richard dropped to his knees and looked where Percival was holding the torch. He could see the gap. "What are you waiting for?" he said.

"This might be how they got out," said Percival, "but there is no way of knowing where it leads to or if it is safe."

"If my son has gone through there, I am going also," and with that, he slid into the gap. He fell through the hole and landed right in front of Stephen and Oliver. Stephen released Oliver's hand; he jumped on his father as he lay on his back. Richard laughed. To have his son back with him again, he could not believe it.

Richard got to his feet and called out to Percival. Because he was right there at the gap, he could hear Richard's faint voice calling, "There is no way we can get back up."

Percival called back, "So what do you want us to do?"

"Go back to the cave and wait. We have tunnels to explore; we will see if any lead back to you." And so, Percival and the guards returned to the cave where they had set up camp.

Richard, Oliver and Stephen were alone; they had between them just two torches and one sword, no food and no water. "Well I guess we had better try one of the tunnels," said Richard. He picked up Oliver in his arms, and Oliver threw his arms around his father's neck and clung on tightly.

Richard had returned his sword to his belt, and Stephen had a torch in each hand. "Let's try this one," said Richard. So Stephen, with both torches, led the way. They didn't get very far before the tunnel got too narrow to continue, so back they went. A cross was placed on the ground at the entrance just as before, so they knew which tunnel they had tried. They moved on to the next one. As they ventured further and further along, they noticed a breeze blowing through the tunnel. This seemed promising. The tunnel was rising all the time, then they heard voices, human voices; they could not believe their luck. They had made it back to the original cave. One of the guards was first to see them exiting the tunnel. He let out a cheer as he saw King Richard, and everyone turned to see them climbing down from the tunnel which was higher than the others.

"Your Majesty," said Percival, "glad to have you back."

"Glad to be back," replied Richard. It had been another exhausting day; they ate and retired to bed early. There's another day tomorrow. It felt as though they were getting nowhere; for two weeks now, they had checked a different tunnel each day, and each one was a disappointment. Finally, the only one left to try was the one that was highest on the wall, the one that led to the cave that Oliver and Stephen had fallen into. One thing had become apparent. If this was the tunnel they were going to use, the wagons would no longer be of any use; they would each have to carry some provisions. They climbed to the entrance of the tunnel and set off; it went down in a slow decline, and before long, they entered the cave; now they had to choose from a number of tunnels. One was already marked with a cross, which they had tried before, so off they set, down yet another passageway. It was narrow, but on foot, they managed with ease, then suddenly, it went into a steep decline. The guard at the front stumbled slightly but managed to stay on his feet. He relayed this back down the line. Everyone was treading carefully. The prince was joined to his father by a rope. The pathway levelled off, and yet another cave opened once more, another high ceiling barely visible by torch, but in front of them now lay four separate passageways. The same two guards who first entered the cave volunteered to check the passages. The king praised them for their courage, and they set off.

They decided to take the passage on the left; after a short while they returned, a dead end. The next passage was the same, no way through. The third passage seemed to go on forever. Then suddenly, from out of the dark, they heard a rustling noise and before they knew what was happening, they were surrounded by a swarm of bats. The two guards fell to the floor as the bats circled above their heads, their wing beats created a cooling breeze above their heads, and then they were gone, flying off down the passageway the guards had used. They got to their feet and carried on. They came to a large black underground pool of water. They searched, but there was no way around. They returned once more and told the king what they had found. So this must be the passage to get them through. They indicated the fourth passage. The decision was made this time; they would all go together but carefully. They were being cautious which was just as well, because not very far down the passageway was a gigantic hole.

"Stop the guards at the front," the guard called. Everyone stopped instantly.

"What is it?" called Richard.

"There's a gigantic hole, Your Majesty, we will have to go back." They felt defeated.

"We need to find another cave," said Percival.

"Yes," said Richard. They decided to rest in the cave for the night and look for another cave in the morning; once again, fires were lit. Stephen asked if he could see the underground pool.

Richard saw no reason to deny the request, and one of the guards said he was willing to go with Stephen. They each carried a torch and arrived safely at the pool. Stephen stepped closer to the pool and as the light from the torch shone on the surface of the black pool of water, a light seemed to appear below the surface, then another and another, and in a matter of seconds there was a huge pool of light at their feet, shining up out of the water. It made the cave sparkle.

"Such beauty in such a dark place," said Stephen. They both looked in awe at the effect the light had on the cave.

Then Stephen remembered something from the story Percival had told them and wanted to return immediately. They made their way back to the cave.

"Percival, in your story do you remember the part in the cave? Did it not say that they found a watery exit, all they had to do was step into the light, almost correct, but I believe it was, and they stepped onto the light. Your Majesty, with your permission, I would like to try something. It is an odd request, I know, but at the pool, when we shone a light over the water, something from beneath rose to the surface—an aquatic animal. There were a lot of them, and they seemed to stop just below the surface, as if joined together to make like a raft, which glowed in the light. In Percival's story, it said step onto the light. I would like, with your permission, to try this idea out."

"Are you sure, boy? This sounds a bit crazy."

"Yes, Your Majesty, think of the creatures we have encountered so far, so many things we have never seen before. I think this might be our way through."

"Very well," said Richard, "you have my permission."

Accompanied by two guards, Stephen went to the pool. With the torches lit, the flames flickered as they shone their torches over the water. As before, the creatures started to gather before them; shining in the torch light, they looked like giant diamonds glowing in the water. Stephen tentatively put a foot forward. He was extremely relieved to feel his weight supported on the surface of the water; he placed his second foot next to his first. It felt stable, but now what? He was speaking with the guards when he said, "How does this help us find a way out?" And with that, the light beneath his feet started to move away from the guards.

One tried to leap onto the light and missed; he fell into the cold water, but the other guard helped him out.

They watched as the young scribe disappeared into the darkness, his torch slowly getting smaller the further he went on his way. Feeling frightened and excited all at the same time, Stephen could not help himself. *What on earth am I going to do now?* he thought. There was no sign of any light ahead, only the torch he carried and the light shining up from the strange creatures beneath his feet.

The two guards had returned to their king, breathing heavily, for they had returned as fast as they could.

They said, "Your Majesty!"

The king looked at them as they were gasping for breath and asked, "Where is Stephen?"

They told their king how Stephen had indeed stepped onto the light, only to be carried away into the blackness. They had watched him disappear, unable to help. Stephen was still riding on the backs of these strange water inhabitants, and the ceiling came into view. It was very low; he had to lay down quickly to avoid hitting the ceiling but as he did, he dropped the torch into the water. As soon as the light had gone, the creatures that had been supporting him at the surface also disappeared. He began to panic but knew he had to calm himself. Taking some deep breaths, he put his hands up and, touching the low ceiling, moved hopefully forwards. He was pleasantly surprised to find he could walk on the bottom and as he moved even forward, the ceiling remained low, but the water was getting even more shallow and before long, he was out of the water; once again, the ceiling had gone out of reach. In complete blackness, for he could not even see his own hands, he decided to sit still and wait, hoping the others would follow. Whilst sitting quietly alone in the pitch black and deafening silence, he had no sense of how long he sat there before he felt a soft breeze on his right arm. He suddenly became aware of the cool air and realised that the air had to be coming from outside. He got on his hands and knees and decided this was the best option for moving. He tentatively placed a hand on the ground, slowly feeling with his hands, unable to see. As he crawled across the floor, it was cold to touch. Following the breeze now on his face and getting stronger, he was careful not to get too carried away. He still could not see anything. Just as well he moved slowly; he put a hand forward, and the invisible floor was not there. He had discovered a hole. He reached with his right hand and found the edge of the hole; he ran his hand around the rim. It was only a small hole but still big enough for an arm to fall into. It was a great reminder to be extra careful in the pitch black. Then suddenly, a glimmer of light pierced the blackness. As he moved forward, light began to illuminate the tunnel, and he escaped from the dark into the bright sunlight. Having been in the pitch black, the glorious sunshine was, for a second, quite blinding. Rubbing his eyes, he soon got used to the light again. He had made it through; what a relief.

The king now had a decision to make: *Do we try to follow Stephen or try to find another way through the mountain?* They had no way of knowing if the young scribe had made it through or not but one of the guards said he was willing to try the same way Stephen had. It was settled; this time, the king went to see for himself what would happen. And so the king and two guards approached the dark pool of water; with a torch in each hand, one of the guards stepped forwards. Like before, as soon as the light spread across the water's shimmering surface, the creatures from the deep started to gather. It was as if the light was a beacon calling them. He placed one foot onto the shimmering light and then the other. Within a matter of seconds, he was moving; he wobbled at first but regained his balance. The king stood watching in awe as the guard riding the shining light moved further away. They called to him, "Can you see anything?"

'Nothing' was the reply, and suddenly, he was gone. He had reached the part where the ceiling was low, and he had to lay down, but this time, he managed to keep one torch out of the water, and so with one torch lit, the creatures carried him all the way beneath the low ceiling, and then the ceiling raised up once more, and he stopped moving. Standing up, he realised that there was solid ground in front of him. They had carried him as far as they could, and he stepped off, no sign of Stephen. He called out, "Stephen, are you there?" No reply. He looked around and noticed the trail on the dirt floor. Someone or something had left this trail, but with no footprints to go by, he could not be sure if it was Stephen, though decided to follow anyway. He came across the hole, but with a torch lighting the way, it was not a problem. It was not long before the light from outside came flooding into the tunnel, and he was soon in the open air once more. He called again, "Stephen, are you here?"

Stephen answered, "Yes here I am," and he appeared from the bushes, carrying a very large egg.

"I can't believe you made it," said the guard.

"I can't believe you followed," laughed Stephen.

"But now what, how de do we let the others know we made it through?"

Stephen said, "I have been thinking about that, and the fact you made it through with a torch has given me an idea. You made it through with a torch; maybe the creatures will come to the torch and take one of us back the other way. Then we can show the others we made it through."

"Okay," said the guard. "I will go but can we have something to eat first?" he continued, looking at the giant egg in Stephen's hand, "I am starving, of course."

They set a fire and placed the egg in the middle. As it started to crack, they removed it from the fire and cracked it open. It tasted great, but now it was time to try out their plan. With the torch relit, the guard and Stephen went back into the cave. Stephen had made himself a new torch from some wood off the forest floor.

Again, they approached the water's edge, nothing. They waited and waited. Just as they had turned away, having given up hope, a small splash came from the black pool, and as they turned and the light from the torches lit up the surface of the water, there they were once more.

Stephen and the guard were smiling at one another. "Right then," said the guard, "here I go, wish me luck." He lay down with his torch just above the surface of the water, and they were off. Stephen sat down, and within seconds, the guard and his shining underwater raft had gone.

Having passed beneath the low ceiling, the guard was standing once more, then something caught his eye. There appeared to be something in the water in front of him, something huge. His raft turned sharply, and he swayed but managed to stay upright. *What the hell is that?* he thought, and then he felt it—a jolt from beneath—and the outer edge to his right broke away. As he was carried along by the remainder of the creatures, he watched as something flew out of the water to crash back down into the pool with a thunderous splash.

Whatever it is, it's attacking the creatures that are carrying us across this pool, he thought and was terrified. He could see the surface of water swirling and without warning, one of the shining creatures flew out of the water right above his head. It crashed onto solid ground at the edge of the pool and as it thrashed about still alive, something rose up out of the water. It was as dark as the black pool, with a long snout and gleaming white teeth that shone in the torch light; it had raised its head out of the water so as to grab the creature from the bank and drag it back into the deep black pool. His heart was racing, his breathing became shallow, his legs began to quiver, and sweat had formed on his brow and was running down the side of his face. He turned his head one way and then the other; no sign of whatever had attacked. Then the creatures stopped and he was so relieved when able to step once more onto solid ground. The remaining creatures dispersed.

Feeling terribly shaken after what had just happened, he walked slowly back to where he knew King Richard would be waiting. When he arrived back at the camp, Richard rushed over, "Tell me, did you get through?"

"Yes, Your Majesty, I did, and I found Stephen, he's alive, but I must warn you of something," and so he told them about the journey across the pool and the low ceiling and the creature that was attacking the ones they were using.

"So there's something in the water that is dangerous. We will have to be prepared in case we are attacked. We will need some spears," Richard ordered the guards to go back to the forest and search for some branches that were straight, so they could be sharpened into spears. They took their knives with them and gathered up many branches. They took these branches back through the tunnel to the cave where King Richard was waiting and then took their knives and sharpened each branch into a point.

"Okay, is everyone ready?" They were, so off to the pool they went. With so many torches being held above the water's surface, shining brighter than ever, more of the creatures appeared than ever before; once again the cave walls sparkled. It was a strange beauty in such a dark place. They tentatively stepped onto the living raft of light. The guards stood towards the edge, spear in one hand, torch in the other; this was thought to be their best chance of seeing if the other creature returned. The king, the prince and Percival all sat in the middle, along with the cook. Although they heard the odd splash and saw the occasional swirl at the water's surface, the journey was swift and uneventful. Passing below the low ceiling and coming out the other side, torches alight, Stephen knew they had made it through. Once they had all stepped from the raft, it dispersed quickly. The guard told Stephen of the creature he had encountered on the way back.

"Thank God you made it," Stephan said. He led the party through the tunnel, making sure no one put a foot into the hole along the way. They had made it through the mountain.

"What a day it's been. We will camp here for the night and move on in the morning," said Richard. Fires were lit for warmth and to keep away any wild animals, for once again they had an unknown forest that sprawled out before them with untold hidden dangers.

Chapter 6
The Princesses

The queen still sat alone in her room, staring out blankly into the garden. The princesses were being entertained by the nannies. All were in the garden playing with their kites. It was quite a windy day, and they were all laughing. Hanging on tightly to their kites, the little princesses seemed not to have a care in the world. The royal physician, on the other hand, was very worried; the queen hadn't eaten anything substantial in the last six days. She was starving herself; with the loss of appetite, it seemed she had lost the will to live. She was in danger of making herself very ill, possibly even killing herself. Something had to be done. He had made the decision to lie to Her Majesty, the queen. He told her that news had been received that the king and Prince Oliver were on their way home and would be back within a week.

This was just the news the queen needed. She asked for some food to be brought to her room; having not eaten properly for six days, she was hungry. She ate what she could. She was suddenly happy again, eager to see her three daughters, but weak, for not having eaten for so long. They would give her a couple of days to build up her strength before bringing the little Princesses in to see her; she agreed to this. She could not believe that Richard was on his way home, and to see Oliver again, what a relief. The physician had lied, but then he worried, what would happen when after a week had passed and there was no sign of King Richard or Prince Oliver. How would the queen react? He had no way of knowing, but for now, she was eating, which was progress. The three little princesses were being kept busy by the nannies; every day, they would take them out riding on their ponies. Each nanny held the reins to one of the dapple grey ponies as they led them around the castle grounds. It was now June, and the sunshine was pleasantly warm. The grounds were in bloom and looked stunning, rabbits could be seen racing across the grass, squirrels were shooting up and down the trees, and birds were in full song; it was idyllic. It seemed as if Alice, Dorothy and Mary had forgotten all about Oliver, but this was not true. They had realised that their mother was unhappy and had used one of the secret passageways that Oliver had shown them; they had listened to their mother talking with the physician, and they knew exactly what was going on. They were even aware that the physician had lied to their mother.

The three young princesses had decided not to question their mother about Oliver so as not to upset her. Anyway, if they listened in secret, they could find out what was going on, and no one would be lying to them.

Chapter 7
Strange Animals

Before entering the forest, King Richard was talking with one of his guards. Oliver was playing with his wooden sword. Percival and Stephen were watching. What was he doing? On closer inspection, Percival could see he had found a small lizard sitting on a rock, enjoying the morning sun.

Stephen asked Percival, "Do you know if that is dangerous?"

"No, quite harmless. But watch," he said.

Oliver was poking at the small lizard with his wooden sword; it began to hiss. Once. Twice. Oliver poked at the lizard and on the third occasion, *puff,* it had inflated a frill that surrounded its head, making itself look much bigger than it actually was and then just as quickly, it had disappeared.

"It's a tactic it uses to surprise any predator. In that moment of surprise is his best chance of escape, for they are lightning fast," Percival explained.

Oliver began to search for the lizard, but it was gone. This forest was the noisiest they had encountered yet, and with lots of strange noises, they knew they had to be cautious. There were large blue birds in huge numbers sitting high in the branches; their loud calls were as unfamiliar as their appearance. There were pools of water everywhere; tall birds with thin legs and long supple necks were wading through the shallows; out in the middle of the pool were birds that kept disappearing beneath the surface, only to reappear a second or two later. They came across some very large footprints; they had no idea what made them, but they were round and had sunk deep into the soft mud around the water's edge. All they could think of was whatever made those prints must have been very large and heavy to have sunk so deep into the soil. This was not very comforting; to think something large was there with them and they had no idea what it was. A loud squeal from the bushes alerted them to something hidden. The Kingsguard were ready with spears and swords, not knowing what to expect. Then a pig appeared and with a sigh, they felt relieved, only to be scared the very next second as a giant snake leapt forth and grabbed the pig. As it squealed and struggled to break free, the snake coiled itself around the pig and crushed it. The sight of the pig being crushed and then eaten had caused the young prince to shed a tear as he clung to his father but still not a sound. They left the snake behind to finish devouring his meal.

Everything was bigger here, the trees were much taller than back home and the exposed roots reminded Stephen of legs, as if the trees could come to life. The trunks of the trees looked ancient, aged with time, maybe a thousand years or more, and the flowers and the leaves of all the plants were huge. Stephen was making notes of everything he saw. As he was looking up at the tallest of the trees, he felt something hit his forehead. It was starting to rain, only this was no ordinary rain, just like everything else in this place. The droplets of rain were large, in fact, very large, and they hurt. They needed to find some shelter and quick; luckily, they had just passed a plant that had resembled a gigantic mushroom; they all huddled together under the canopy provided by this massive plant. A clap of thunder boomed overhead, again, much louder than anything they were used to, and the intensity of the lightning was almost blinding as it streaked across the sky. As the thunder claps roared, the lighting strikes streaked from the sky to the ground, a cracking noise could be heard. A large tree had been hit as they watched a large branch break away from the trunk and a third of the tree crash to the ground. The wind had also picked up and was driving the rain horizontally. The canopy of the massive plant was no longer any use for shelter; the ground was becoming waterlogged fast. They had to move and find somewhere dry. As the rain continued to pour, the temperature had dropped. Also, if the temperature continued to drop overnight, they would need a fire for warmth; they had to move. Using their swords like axes, the guards attempted to chop off some leaves for cover, so they could move.

"But, Your Majesty, these stems are as tough as an oak tree," they explained.

"Let me try," said Richard. As his sword hit the thick stem, the vibration coursed its way through his entire body. "Well, that's not going to work," he said. They would have to go back to the cave. Stephen thought he knew the way because he had been writing everything down he had observed. But everything looked different now; with the rain pouring down, the giant flowers had closed tightly, the leaves of the ferns had recoiled into balls and one plant with long slender leaves had pulled its leaves into an upright position so that it now resembled a giant spear.

They had to move, but which direction? Someone laughed. No, they must have imagined it! No, there it was again, and with a big grin, Dante, the winged fairy, stood before them. He was standing at the base of the tallest tree. There seemed to be a light behind Dante, coming from inside the tree, and he was beckoning them. After what happened the last time they saw the fairy, the king was understandably reluctant, but looking at his young son in his arms, he made a run for it; everyone else followed. Even though it was only thirty paces from their shelter to the tree, they were soaked through to the skin. "Are you sure this is safe?" Richard asked Dante.

"Yes, Your Majesty, this tree is quite resistant to lightning."

Inside the tree was a fire, and it was so warm and welcoming after being stuck out in the rain. They were all gathered around the fire, their clothes sending up steam like from an overgrown stew pot. It was Dante who spoke, "Welcome, Your Majesty, I told you we would meet again," and he bowed. Everyone was grateful to Dante, but they were suspicious. He sat on a stump, away from them and the fire, and observed. Percival was looking around, it was truly amazing, and it was just like being back inside the cave. It was a vast space.

Percival asked Dante, "How and why?"

Dante simply replied, "The rain."

King Richard approached Dante, bowed and said, "Thank you."

Dante smiled, "Where is Berwyn?"

Percival told him of the strange creature called Ossirus and how he had managed to steal Berwyn. "They are called Matsuba," said Dante. "They are usually a peaceful race. I wonder why he wanted Berwyn." This conversation held no interest for King Richard, and so he returned to his young son by the fire. With the storm still raging outside, they finally fell asleep. In the morning, when they awoke, the embers of the fire were still glowing but no sign of Dante.

"Damn this fairy," said Richard, "he has a habit of disappearing. I don't like it." Stephen said he had been the first of them to wake up, and Dante had already left. Before they were all awake, Stephen asked Percival about the rest of the story. Now they had managed to get through the mountain, what was the next thing to look out for? "That would be the river of a thousand deaths," said Percival.

"Oh, that sounds wonderful," said Stephen.

Percival said, "I believe we follow the sun, from sunrise to sunset. We had better wake everyone up then and make a start."

With everyone awake and having spoken with the king about what they were to look for next, they stepped out of the tree. "Good morning, Your Majesty." It was Dante. He had prepared a breakfast for the party. "Please have something to eat before you leave." Not wanting to offend the fairy, they all sat and ate. He asked the king about their journey, and as before, the king's answer was vague for he still did not want Dante to know the purpose of their journey.

Instead, the king asked Dante, "What are you doing here?"

Dante answered as vaguely as the king, "Oh I like to get around, visit new places." They eyed each other with suspicion.

One of the guards spoke, "I think it is time we were on our way, Your Majesty."

"Yes, I think it is time we left." He thanked Dante for his help and said, "I hope you find what you are looking for."

Dante replied, "I will." And with that, he was gone.

It was hot again now they were out of the mountain but not as hot as the desert had been. There were butterflies the size of a crow, with vivid bright colours. Richard asked for some to be caught. He knew his daughters back home would love to see them, but they had nothing big enough to put them in, so Stephen drew some detailed pictures instead.

On they went following the sun, with no pathways. They had to cut their way through the smaller bushes to keep moving forward. They stopped; there was something blocking their way. "What is that?" asked one of the guards. It was hanging from the trees above and was milky white, like a giant piece of lace, but it was everywhere. They didn't have to wait long. Suspended on a single white lace thread was a giant spider; it slowly lowered itself to the floor in front of them, picked up something and began to ascend once more, back up to its lace web.

"We need to get out of here now," said King Richard.

As they moved under the giant web, they looked up and could see why the web was so big: there were huge spiders everywhere; some were eating while some seemed to be sleeping. They had almost passed beneath the web when three spiders dropped right into their path. With swords drawn, the guards battled the giant spiders, trying to avoid the pincers. As the fight raged on, Richard, carrying Oliver, passed by quickly, followed by Percival, Stephen and the cook. One of the guards quickly lit a torch and thrust it into the face of one of the spiders; it retreated for a second but soon re-joined the fight. The guard with the torch attacked another of the spiders but this time set alight the spider web. It spread quickly, so now they were fighting these huge spiders underneath a canopy of burning web. At this point, one guard came forward with a spear and threw it, killing one of the spiders; the other two started fighting each other over the dead body.

"Cannibalism," said Percival.

The guards quickly moved from underneath the burning web. Looking back, they saw the whole web ablaze, and the large clump of trees that supported the giant web was also on fire. The heat was intense. There was a shallow but wide stream; they crossed quickly to safety from the inferno they had created. They had left the trees only to find themselves in the tallest grass they had ever seen. It was so tall they could not see where they were going, at all; this was even worse than any forest. With the heat from the sun and the dampness of the grass, there was a mist lurking overhead menacingly. They could hear rustling noises coming from the grass and from all sides; they were surrounded. They had no idea what it was that had them surrounded. As panic was setting in and with swords drawn, they waited apprehensively, when out from the long grass came the smallest of ducks, or what looked like ducks, but at the same time, unlike anything else they had seen. They were dull green in colour with large bulbous eyes and blue beaks; they blended perfectly with the long grass. They walked straight past the king's party, searching for grubs on the ground. Then something strange happened. They were startled, and they all ran together, formed a circle, some jumped onto the backs of others and so on, forming a huge tower of snapping little beaks. There must have been easily a hundred, maybe more. It was only then they could see that the innocent-looking, little duck-like creatures had needle sharp teeth. And then it appeared: a small cat like creature, stalking, slowly circling the ducks looking for a weak spot. So engrossed in its hunt, it never even noticed the king's party. It was now crouching, getting ready to pounce, when suddenly, without warning, it was the cat-like creature's turn to be startled. A loud crashing noise was moving at speed through the tall grass. With a loud squawking noise, two very long-legged birds appeared, and the cat fled. Now the two birds turned their attention to the king's party; they dare not run because they knew they wouldn't get more than a couple of steps before they would be caught.

Richard said, "Don't move, stay where you are; if they see we're no threat, they won't attack." Stephen and Percival looked at each other, beads of sweat running down Percival's cheek. Neither looked too convinced by what Richard said, but as they stood completely still, the two giant birds had calmed and the youngsters had dismounted and were back on the ground searching out grubs. They moved away through the tall grass.

The party could breathe once more. The cook said to Stephen, "Did you see the size of its legs?" They both laughed with relief.

Having struggled through the long grass for most of the morning, at midday with the sun at its highest point, they were once again out in the open. In the distance, they could see a group of four animals that at first glance resembled a deer from back home. Two guards took out a bow and arrow; they crept forward as quietly as possible so as not to scare the animals off. One of the creatures closest to them had been grazing, and when it raised its head, they could clearly see that this was nothing like a deer from back home. It had horns instead of antlers, and they were covered in blood, and it was not grazing on grass as they had previously thought; it was, in fact, eating the flesh of another large animal, judging by the blood on its horns, an animal that it had killed. They stared at each other; the animal put its head down and carried on with its meal. The guards were unsure of what to do.

They returned to King Richard. "I think its best we try to avoid confrontation with this animal. There are four and judging by the size of the animal they have killed, they are extremely dangerous." The animals, busy eating, did not give the king's party a second look but continued to gorge themselves on their kill. King Richard and his party moved on. They arrived at a narrow river, no more than twelve feet across, but the banks down to the river were quite steep.

"This, I believe," said Percival, "is the river of a thousand deaths."

"How did it get that name?" asked Stephen.

"The current is said to be so strong that any animal that tries to cross gets swept away and drowned," Percival replied. This seemed unlikely, as the surface of the water seemed practically motionless. "We need to find a safer place to get down to the water before we attempt to cross." And so they followed the river as it snaked its way across the land. Flying high overhead was a single large bird, soaring across the sky, riding the warm air currents as it gracefully glided on by. It landed a short distance away; in flight, it had appeared graceful, but once on the ground, its extremely large wings made movement cumbersome and awkward. It had found an old carcass and began feeding; then a second and third large bird arrived, and they began to squabble over the carcass. The one who had arrived first was slightly smaller than the other two and was driven off, but as he had been the first to arrive, he had eaten enough. There was no point in him fighting the larger birds for mere scraps. After witnessing this, Richard and his party moved on, still searching for an easier place to cross. It was late afternoon when they came across a large number of footprints leading down to the river. The bank was not as steep as before and so made the river more accessible. One of the guards volunteered to attempt to cross the river; he made his way down to the water's edge and started out.

"It's fine," he called as he looked back. Then a couple of steps further and he was in trouble. So suddenly had it happened, he was caught unawares. He had gone under, then his head bobbed at the surface and he was being thrown about, thrashing his arms to stay on top of the water. He went under again; the surface of the water was now a raging rapid. His screams were drowned out by the noise of the river. Helplessly, they could do nothing but watch him get carried away; they followed the river and hoped that it would calm down, and they would find him alive. Judging by the way he was being tossed around, they didn't hold much hope for his survival. As they followed the river, it seemed to calm down, but as they rounded a bend, it picked up again, more violent than before, then it disappeared. They had reached a waterfall. The king and one guard approached where the river went over the edge. They looked down; it was a huge drop. They knew that no one could survive a fall like that, but they still wanted to find the body.

They made their way down and found a huge pool, and to one side, they could see the crumpled body of the guard. They retrieved his body so they could bury him. The river continued its way, slicing a pathway through the countryside, as innocent looking as any river back home. How would they get across? They kept following the river in the hope it would become so shallow they could cross or indeed come across some sort of bridge. They found neither that day. Percival was adamant that this was the river they needed to cross, but it was getting dark, so they decided to set up camp. Fires were lit to keep away any wild animals. All through the night, they could hear strange noises in the dark. They were next to the water so they knew that this meant animals would come for a drink. In the morning, they were surprised to see just how many footprints there were around their camp and just how close some of the animals had come to the fires.

The king's party were on the move, still searching for a way to cross the river. They found a huge number of carcasses of dead animals. "So this is the reason it's called the river of a thousand deaths," said Richard. Never had they seen anything like the sight that was before them: animals of various sizes, all intertwined with legs and horns; birds sat on top of the carcasses eating the flesh. There was no need to squabble because plenty of food here.

One of the guards had an idea. "Your Majesty, look." He had pointed out that where the bodies were laid, they had formed a blockage, and on the other side, the water was shallower but seemed to stretch as far as the eye could see. "Do you think we can cross here?"

Remembering what the river looked like when they first saw it, the king was apprehensive. Percival reminded him of the story and where the bodies lay so the water calms. "This must be the place; we will attempt the crossing." But he was still a little scared, even though he didn't show it, for he carried Oliver in his arms. They stumbled on some bones that littered the shallow water, but the water did not rage as before, which was just as well for the crossing took them all afternoon, and it was starting to get dark as they made it to the other side. Once out of the water, they moved away quite a distance; they thought it was best not to be too close to the water just in case any animals come for a drink, considering how close they came to the fires last night. So once again, fires were lit, but this time two guards were to stay awake and swap over when they were too tired. Prince Oliver was tied to his father, who lay with his arms wrapped around his son for safety. Percival, Stephen and the cook lay together near to one of the fires, while the guards were spread out around the camp; the two who were awake each held a spear in one hand and a sword in the other, just in case.

It was late into the night before anything happened. One guard asked the other, "Did you see that?"

The other replied, "I thought I saw something move in the shadows, but I'm not sure."

As they both stared out into the blackness of night, three sets of eyes stared back at them. "There." One of the guards had spotted them. Suddenly, everyone was waking up, as three large, cat-like animals began to approach. They were cautious of the fires. Now all the guards stood together, with swords and spears; the large cats started to circle the camp, looking for any weakness in the defence. The guards circled with them, face-to-face; the tension was rising knowing that an attack could happen at any moment. Richard held Oliver in his arms for safety, and the attack was launched. One of the cats broke away from the other two and ran straight at the guards. As the guards were distracted, the other two cats circled in opposite directions. One ran through a gap in the fires and was inside the camp; snarling and baring giant white fangs, he was closing in on King Richard, who was still holding Prince Oliver. Percival stepped in front of the cat.

101

Stephen wondered if Percival could stop it, having seen what Percival had done in the past, but this time, it seemed Percival had no control over the cat. It was up to Stephen. He had a spear in his hand. He couldn't even remember picking it up, but he launched the spear, and it hit the target just as the cat had pounced and fell on top of Percival. Richard gave Oliver to the cook and raced over to the cat and lifted its limp body as Stephen pulled Percival from under the cat.

Now with two cats left, the guards had split, and once again, each group was face to face with one of the cats. This time, they launched a coordinated attack: they both raced forward at the same time, but it turned out one was not as brave as the other; as the guards launched their spears, one decided it was too great a risk and ran off. So now only one was left. This remaining cat was the largest of the three. It was moving slowly, observing, circling, weighing up its options and then quite by surprise, it disappeared back into the night. No one slept.

"A beautiful sunrise," said Stephen to Percival. "Let's hope we have a good day."

Before them spread a vast grassy plain, with huge herds of animals. At first glance, some looked like the cows back home but were much bigger and coloured in individual patterns of various bright colours.

"Nothing like the cows back home," remarked Stephen as he quickly made some drawings. But the grass and shrubs they were feeding on were brightly coloured as well, and so they blended together. There was one long-legged species that had a bright red and yellow striped face and neck, black body that was covered in small white spots, with orange and yellow striped legs, so when it was standing its legs seemed to disappear, and its body seemed to be floating as it extended its long neck to reach up into the trees for the leaves it was eating. But when this animal sat down, its neck and head seemed to disappear, and its black body covered in small white spots resembled the large boulders on the ground, perfectly blending in, most peculiar. And birds with an enormous wingspan flew overhead; from underneath, they were the colour of the blue sky and almost invisible, but once on the ground, they had plumage to rival the colours of the herbivores, very bright and gaudy. They had found the carcass of a large dead animal and were picking at the last remaining bits of flesh on its bones.

"This is a savage land," remarked Stephen.

Richard asked Percival what they could expect to find next, now that they had crossed the river of a thousand deaths.

"Well the story speaks of an ancient kingdom and a jewelled tiger, a jewelled tiger," said Stephen. "Yes, we must find this kingdom and make an offering to the tiger."

"But how do we find such a kingdom?" At that very moment, they felt the earth shake. This had happened before, so they knew what to expect next, and out of the ground popped a creature that looked exactly like Ossirus.

"My name is Anteaus," he said.

Anteaus might have looked like Ossirus, but he certainly wasn't dressed like him. Where Ossirus was dressed in nothing more than rags, Anteaus was dressed in a red and gold patterned robe; where Ossirus had bare feet, Anteaus was wearing deep purple shoes on his feet that curled up at the toes. Where Ossirus's appearance was skeletal, Anteaus, although still thin, was much healthier looking. He wasn't carrying a spear either but a walking cane that looked solid gold.

The king approached Anteaus, "My name is King Richard."

Anteaus bowed, "Your Majesty, and what has brought you to my kingdom?" he asked.

The king spoke with Anteaus, telling him of the story and the journey they had undertaken to find the green-striped zebra. Anteaus listened intently without comment until Richard mentioned that they had come across Ossirus. Anteaus immediately reacted. "What did he tell you?" he demanded. King Richard was startled by the sudden change in Anteaus. He was standing, but where he had appeared friendly at first, his stance was now more menacing. Without warning, more creatures appeared, surrounding the King's party, "Tell me, what did Ossirus say to you?"

Percival said, "He didn't tell us anything, but they did steal my bear."

"What kind of bear?" asked Anteaus.

"A white bear," said Percival.

Anteaus was looking a little uneasy, "What size is the bear?"

"He is a giant bear," said Percival. Whispering among themselves, all the creatures surrounding the king's party seemed nervous.

Anteaus had calmed himself. He told them that Ossirus was trying to take over his kingdom. "Ossirus is my brother. When our father died, I was next in line for the throne, but Ossirus challenged me for it. I would not accept his challenge, so he tried to take it by force. He was easily defeated, his followers were quick to surrender, and so he was banished forever. Since being exiled, he has tried on numerous occasions to challenge for the kingdom, but each time, he has failed."

"But why would he want Berwyn?" asked Percival.

"There is a prophecy of a small child riding a giant white bear, who will overthrow the king and claim the throne for himself."

All eyes were now on Oliver; the king realised this. "You cannot think that my son has anything to do with your prophecy. He knows nothing of your kingdom or this bear, and he certainly has never ridden Berwyn."

Anteaus was no longer listening to what King Richard was saying. With a snap of his fingers, they all sank beneath the surface and found themselves in a large underground tunnel, "Follow me," he said. There were torches lit all along the tunnel walls which glowed a golden yellow. Richard went to protest but found the tip of a spear resting against each side of his body; one of Anteaus's followers was leading Oliver by the hand. All of Richard's men had had their weapons taken from them; they followed Anteaus in single file through the tunnel. Suddenly, it opened into a vast space; there were steps leading further underground and down they went. Painted walls showed pictures of strange-looking animals; some they recognised from what they had seen recently, but some were unknown to them. As they approached the bottom of the steps, the ground levelled off. Anteaus stopped. He turned to face King Richard. He pointed to the right, "This is my palace, and on the opposite side is our temple."

"Is that where you make your offering to the jewelled tiger?" Stephen asked.

Anteaus was caught off-guard for a split second. "What do you know of the jewelled tiger?" he asked.

"Only that we need to make an offering."

"Where did you learn of this tiger?"

Percival answered, "It was I who told them of the jewelled tiger."

"And who are you?" asked Anteaus.

"I am just a travelling story teller," answered Percival. "My stories have been passed down to me by my ancestors for generations. We do not know how much truth there is in them, maybe none." Percival didn't really believe this, for everything so far in his story had happened.

"There is no such thing as a jewelled tiger," said Anteaus. Percival knew that was a lie, for if the tiger did not exist, Anteaus would not have been so quick to ask how they knew of its existence.

Anteaus asked King Richard to join him in a tour of the palace. The rest of Richard's party were shown to a large room where they would be staying. As they stepped inside, the doors were quickly closed behind them; the guards tried to open them, but the doors held firm.

"It seems we are prisoners," said Percival. The palace was unlike anything Richard had encountered before: there were torches on all the walls for light. In the centre of the room they were in was a huge fountain; it looked as though it was made of gold.

"I know what you are thinking," said Anteaus, "and yes, it is pure gold, why I have never seen anything like it before in my life and probably never will again," he continued. He led Richard down a passageway into another room. "This is where my wives stay, there is a pool for bathing, and silk curtains hang from ceiling to floor, and behind there are their sleeping quarters," said Anteaus. Once more, Richard was let into another room and an even larger pool; this was for Anteaus and entertaining guests. There was a large area of cushions on the floor. Anteaus gestured to Richard to sit down. As they did, Anteaus clicked his fingers and a group of females dressed in bright gold clothing appeared, carrying what turned out to be trays of food.

When they lowered the trays and Richard could see what was being offered, he declined. Anteaus asked, "Are you not hungry after your journey? I have had prepared all the delicacies that we have to offer." Richard looked again; all he could see was a plate of fire worms and slugs and some other things that he had no idea what they were, but everything was still alive and moving.

Richard asked, "How is it you can eat fire worms?"

"I'm surprised you know what they are," said Anteaus. "If you soak them in water, it cools them down." He picked up a handful of fire worms, held them up in the air and opened his mouth; he tilted his head back and just dropped them in. Richard sat watching as Anteaus went for a second handful, "You really should try them, you know." Richard felt sick but decided he should try them so as not to offend his host. They wriggled inside his mouth, and his first thought was to spit them back out, but not wanting to offend Anteaus, he chewed them as quickly as possible. Anteaus was right; the water had cooled them enough to be able to eat them, but they still tasted awful. He swallowed.

Anteaus clicked his fingers and the females left, only to be followed by a different group wearing red clothing, carrying more trays. Richard wondered what was being offered this time. As they lowered the trays, Richard was pleasantly surprised to see meat, that was, until he realised that it was raw. Anteaus picked up a large piece of meat with both hands and began tearing off chunks of meat with his teeth, dripping blood everywhere. "Why are you not eating? I thought this would be more to your liking." Richard leant forward and picked up the smallest piece he could find, fully aware Anteaus was watching his every move. The blood from the meat was running down his fingers. He placed it into his mouth and ripped a small piece off and was pleasantly surprised. It tasted so much better than it looked. Richard helped himself to a second piece. Anteaus smiled and nodded. When they had finished, he clicked his fingers once more. The females wearing red retreated only to be replaced by a third group wearing the same outfits as before except now they were blue. Once more, they lowered the trays in front of Anteaus and Richard. "I hope you like these," said Anteaus. "They are a real speciality." All Richard could see was a plate full of live snails. As Anteaus picked one off the tray, Richard turned his head. He heard the brittle shell of the snail crack and knew Anteaus had placed it into his mouth; only when the crunching sound had ended did Richard dare turn his head once more to look at his host, Anteaus was smiling. "I guess this is not to your liking," he said.

"I do not mean to offend you," said Richard.

"I am not offended," said Anteaus. "You are not the first to find our delicacies not to your taste." Anteaus clicked his fingers once more, and the trays were taken away.

Richard asked, "So how long have you lived underground?"

Anteaus replied, "Many generations ago, there was a devastating fire, and the safest place for our ancestors was to retreat underground. Over the years that followed, the palace was created, followed by the temple. We can go above ground for the food we eat and collect our water in underground pools."

"Tell me more of your brother Ossirus," asked Richard.

"Ossirus wants to claim the throne and take our people back above ground, to reclaim the land that used to belong to us and return to our old way of life."

"So why don't you return above ground?"

"The old way of living was what brought about our demise in the first place. It was a fight amongst our own people that caused the great fire. Here, underground, we have safety and water; food is easily collected from above. There is no greed or envy amongst us anymore."

Anteaus rose from the cushions and Richard followed. "Let me show you some of our finest possessions." Anteaus led the way. He clapped his hands and two guards appeared; they followed Anteaus and King Richard. The first room they entered was a gold tomb of Anteaus and Ossirus' father and mother; there were shelves cut into the walls displaying gold plates and goblets covered with jewels, and there was gold jewellery mounted with precious stones. There was a doorway to the rear which led to a smaller room; this tomb contained the three priests who had served his father. There were ceremonial goblets covered in precious jewels and ceremonial robes hanging on the wall, and beyond this room was a third. "This is the room where all our wealth is held; no one from outside has ever seen this room before."

"You honour me," said Richard as he followed Anteaus, eager to see what was in this third room. As Richard entered the room, Anteaus stood to one side. Indeed, King Richard had never set eyes on such a room. This room was by far the biggest, and the centre of the room was dominated by a golden chariot, but everywhere there were treasures, gold necklaces adorned with precious jewels, gold vases, plates, statues of animals, all made of solid gold, even the weapons were made of gold. Anteaus pointed out to Richard, "These are the treasures that have been collected over many centuries. Many an empire has fallen before us; our warriors were legendary." Anteaus was very proud of this room and the room seemed to go on forever. Richard turned to Anteaus, who was smiling at him.

"You were right," Richard said. "I have never seen such a collection."

"You must be tired. Get some rest, and we will talk again in the morning."

Richard followed the guards down a narrow tunnel. As they approached a doorway, one of the guards stepped to one side as the other opened the door. "We hope you will be comfortable here, Your Majesty." Richard stepped into a room. There was nothing but a pile of cushions on the floor. As he looked around, the door was quickly shut behind him. He ran to the door and tried to push it open, but it was locked.

He called to the guards for an explanation; there was no answer. Angry and annoyed, he paced around the room, searching for another way out. "Why have they done this?" he said to himself, and his thoughts went to his son and the rest of his party. Eventually, he sat down; his anger slowly dissipated. Wondering what was going on, he slowly fell asleep.

Above ground, Ossirus was sitting with Berwyn. He had some strange control over the giant bear. He was not tied and made no attempt to escape; he seemed perfectly content. He lay at his feet just as he did with Percival. Suddenly, from nowhere, a small child-like figure appeared. Ossirus and his followers watched as the figure approached. This small child-like figure was wearing green clothing and had transparent wings; it was Dante the fairy. He introduced himself. "My name is Dante," he said.

Ossirus stood and asked, "What are you doing here?"

"I have travelled a long way and seek a safe place to rest. May I join you?"

With a wave of his hand, Ossirus gestured for Dante to sit down. "My name is Ossirus."

Dante wasted no time in asking, "What a magnificent beast; where did you find him?" He was referring to Berwyn.

Ossirus lied, "We have had him from when he was small, many years now."

"I have been following King Richard and his men," said Dante. Ossirus realised straight away Dante knew they were lying about the length of time they had had Berwyn.

"Why have you been following King Richard?" asked Ossirus.

"I have been trying to persuade him to let me have the giant bear," said Dante.

"What is your reason for wanting this bear?" asked Ossirus.

"I believe he can carry me to great wealth," said Dante. Ossirus was beginning to show interest.

"I believe if we work together, we can both get what we want. I have heard of a prophecy of a child riding a giant white bear that can overthrow a kingdom." Ossirus's eyes lit up.

"What if the child was not actually a child but a small child-like fairy?"

This was interesting to Ossirus. "But what do you want?" he asked.

"You can have your kingdom and power," said Dante. "I would just like a share of the wealth. And I know I can help."

"How?" said Ossirus.

"I know you are greatly outnumbered, and in battle, many lives would be lost, but what if I could help prevent those deaths?"

"And how is that possible?" Dante then told Ossirus of a special tree. When there is a forest fire and this tree feels the heat from the fire, it releases a sap from within which coats the whole tree; the sap hardens in the air and protects the tree from the flames. A week or so later, the sap peels away, leaving the tree completely unharmed. "If we can create enough heat to make the tree produce sap, we can cover ourselves; the hardened shell will protect against spear or blade. But the shell does not restrict movement."

"Are you sure about this?" asked Ossirus.

"Yes, of course. I can take you where I know there is a group of these trees; it will take a couple of days to get there and back."

And so it was decided. Dante would help Ossirus regain his kingdom, and Ossirus would give Dante his reward.

A couple of days had passed. Anteaus went to his temple to speak with three holy men who resided there. They talked of the prophecy, the young prince and the giant white bear. They were convinced that the prophecy that had been foretold centuries before was about to happen. Anteaus was disturbed. They had to find a way of stopping the prophecy from happening, but the question was how. The one thing that was in their favour was that the young prince was being held in one of his rooms. But then again, Ossirus had stolen the bear from them and now had him in his possession. Anteaus went with two guards to see King Richard, who was not happy about being held prisoner.

Anteaus apologised. "I find myself in a difficult situation, and I am not sure how we can stop the prophecy from happening." Richard tried to assure Anteaus that Oliver had nothing to do with the prophecy but had to admit, his son and Berwyn did fit the prophecy.

Suddenly, out of nowhere, there was a lot of shouting and screaming. "What is that?" asked Richard. They both left the room with the two guards; there was thick black smoke pouring through the tunnels. The Matsuba people were running everywhere.

Richard's thoughts were for his son and the rest of his party. "Anteaus, where is my son?" He pointed to a tunnel opposite. Richard ran in the direction Anteaus had indicated. He found a door and started pounding on it, calling for his son.

Percival was the first to answer, "Yes we are all here."

Richard struggled to remove the heavy bar that was holding the door locked, but with encouragement from within the room, he slowly managed to lift it; it crashed onto the floor, and everyone inside was able to get out. "Quick, we need to leave," he said, but as they exited the room, no one was to be seen; they had all vanished. The smoke was beginning to sting their eyes.

"Where have they all gone?" said Stephen.

"I imagine they've gone above ground," said Percival.

"Then we need to find a way out." Stephen pointed to the left beyond the fountain, "Look, there are steps leading upwards; maybe that is a way out." Richard picked up Oliver, and they all ran towards the steps. The smoke behind them was thick and spreading. They raced up the stairs. Percival stumbled and was helped back to his feet by one of the guards. The stairs seemed to go on forever, but eventually, they had reached a doorway. It opened, and they were relieved to be back above ground. Looking around, they realised they were on top of a hill; all the Matsuba people were gathered below.

Richard was wondering why Anteaus would choose to live underground. With all the skills his people had to create this underground kingdom, surely, they could build themselves a new kingdom above ground. Thousands of Matsuba were now out in the open. For many, this was their first time above ground; it was scary but fascinating at the same time to see the blue sky, the bright sun and to feel the warmth of the sun and the soft breeze; it was amazing. For years, they had been hiding underground. They had been told it was not safe to come above ground. They had been led to believe that it was all on fire and totally uninhabitable. Now they could see for themselves this was not the case. They were talking among themselves, getting agitated. 'How is this possible', 'what is going on?' they were asking. 'Why have we been hidden away underground for so long?', 'why are we not living free, above ground?'

Before Anteaus could answer, in the distance, a tall figure was approaching. Followers of Anteaus were chanting, holding their spears above their heads in a gesture of defiance. The great white bear appeared, and riding on its back was a small child. One of the holy men had been the first to see what was happening; he moved quickly to Anteaus and pointed out, "You see, the prophecy is coming true." Someone overheard what the holy man had said and looked in the direction he was pointing. The news spread like a fire carried on a strong breeze. 'The prophecy is happening, the prophecy is happening,' everyone knew of the prophecy. They watched as the giant white bear moved even closer. The small child-like figure was now visible: wearing green clothing as usual, it was Dante, and walking beside Berwyn was Ossirus. Some of the Matsuba started to cheer; followers from both sides started to clash. Berwyn howled a cry like no one had heard before. The fighting stopped. A chill had run down the spine of Anteaus at the sound of Berwyn. His supporters, fearful of the giant white bear, watched in horror as he walked past; the sheer size of the beast was terrifying. Ossirus, with one hand on Berwyn's neck, made it clear to everyone that the giant white bear was loyal to him. The whole of the Matsuba tribe were transfixed by the child-like figure that rode on the back of the giant white bear. They had never seen a winged fairy before and were intrigued by its appearance. As Ossirus made his way towards his brother Anteaus, the crowds of people parted to make way. Before long, the whole of the kingdom was cheering at the sight of Ossirus. King Richard and his party, on top of the hill, were greeted by this spectacle. They had no idea there were so many of the Matsuba living underground. As the Matsuba parted to let Ossirus pass, Percival spotted Ossirus walking along side Berwyn. He wanted to call to his old friend, but Richard stopped him; he was interested to watch what was happening.

Ossirus walked straight up to Anteaus. A spear was thrown into the ground; the challenge was made. All the followers of both Anteaus and Ossirus stepped back. A giant ring was formed as the two brothers prepared to fight; each was given a spear and a knife. They moved around the ring, facing each other, waiting for the right moment to throw their spear. Ossirus stumbled. This was the moment Anteaus had been waiting for, and he threw his spear but missed. Ossirus was on his feet again; the advantage was now with him. Anteaus was looking around the ring for support; he knew he was in trouble. Ossirus moved as if to throw his spear, and Anteaus ducked. Ossirus had anticipated the move and threw his spear; his spear clipped Anteaus on the side of his chest. Now both of them were armed with only their knives. Anteaus lunged forward and struck Ossirus on the arms, but with the covering of sap which had dried clear, the blade bounced off, leaving so sign of injury. Everyone present gasped; they did not understand what had just happened. Anteaus was one of those who had no idea what was going on. He attacked again. This time, Ossirus made no attempt to defend himself and again, although the blade struck Ossirus right across his chest, there was no visible injury. Dante rode Berwyn in a circle as the two brothers fought; no one dared to intervene. With Berwyn by Ossirus' side and Dante riding the giant white bear, Anteaus conceded defeat. He fell to his knees before his brother. Richard was puzzled. This seemed very strange, but they watched without making a sound, fascinated by what was unfolding before their very eyes. Ossirus climbed onto a large rock so he was visible to everyone. He removed the cloth that covered the top half of his body, and there on his stomach were the markings of a jewelled tiger; everyone fell to their knees and started to chant. He saw King Richard high up on the hill as he looked down. Ossirus dismounted the rock.

He walked past Anteaus who was still kneeling, but as he passed, Anteaus grabbed a spear from one of his followers and meant to throw it into the back of his brother, but a follower of Ossirus who was standing with Berwyn had seen what was happening and threw his own spear into the left leg of Anteaus, who screamed with pain and fell to the ground. Ossirus looked back briefly and then went over to King Richard, who had come down from his vantage point on top of the hill.

"What just happened?" he asked.

"Your Majesty," he said, "my name is Ossirus. Welcome to my kingdom.

Anteaus was carried away. Percival was pleased to see Berwyn again and the great white bear greeted him eagerly, nearly knocking him off his feet. Dante rolled off Berwyn's back and floated above the floor. "I told you we would meet again," he said and smiled.

King Richard was confused. "So just what happened?" he asked Ossirus.

"Anteaus and I are brothers," he said, "but I am the eldest. When our father died, I was the one who should have taken our father's place, but Anteaus used force to take the kingdom. It is law amongst our people that when the leader dies, if there is no son or daughter to take his place, two people can challenge to rule. Only the two wanting to rule must fight, with no interference. The loser must leave, and no one is allowed to go with them. Anteaus challenged my birth right to rule and broke this law when two of his followers helped him to defeat me. Everyone was too scared to stand up to him after that, so I have been in exile, waiting for a chance to reclaim my kingdom. When I saw you with your giant white bear, I remembered the prophecy I had been told many years before I knew this was my chance to get my kingdom back. I needed the bear. I knew with Berwyn by my side nobody would dare challenge me for they fear the prophecy."

"What is the prophecy?" asked Richard.

"The prophecy states that a child riding a giant white bear will overthrow the kingdom; it also says that anyone who stands against them will meet a painful death, and so, when I stood on the rock and revealed the jewelled tiger markings on my stomach, they knew I was the rightful ruler, for each firstborn child has these markings placed onto them by the holy men in the temple. Only they would have known I was the first born."

Richard looked at Percival and asked, "Did not your story say we have to make an offering to the jewelled tiger?"

"Yes, Your Majesty that is exactly what it says."

Ossirus said, "You have helped me regain my kingdom. What is it you want to ask of me?"

"How can we find the green-striped zebra?"

"Oh, that is easy. When the sun sets tonight, I will take you to the pool of magic where the green-striped zebra is said to drink, but legend says he will only come out for the pure of heart."

As the sun set, Ossirus and six of his followers led the way. King Richard and his party followed and Dante followed behind, unseen. Ossirus stopped.

"Only the boy can approach the pool. If more than one person is present at the pool, he will not reveal himself."

And so, Oliver walked forward. It was now moonlight which shone onto the water and as he waited, a zebra approached. But it was just a black and white zebra. Then, as it stepped into the water, something magical happened; with the light reflecting from the surface of the pool, the black stripes were now sparkling green. The young prince was so surprised by this beautiful sight, he spoke his first ever word: "Wow."

The young prince then heard a voice speak to him, "You may have one wish and one wish only; use it wisely."

There was only one thing the young prince wanted and that was to be home with his mother and sisters, and so the wish was made. He returned to his father and told him what had just happened. Richard was so shocked and surprised to hear his son talking, he hadn't heard what Oliver had said. Tears of joy were streaming down his face, and he held his son in a tight embrace. Back at the pool, Dante had silently approached the zebra which was still standing in the water.

Dante said, "I can see you, now grant me my wish."

"And what is your wish?"

"I wish to be sat upon a mountain of gold."

"You shall have your wish," said the zebra, and he turned away from Dante and left the pool.

The next morning, Richard woke early, only to find himself in familiar surroundings. At first, he thought he was dreaming, but rubbing his eyes, he realised he was, in fact, in his own bed in the castle. *This cannot be*, he thought. He got out of bed, put on a robe and made his way to the queen's chambers. The two guards were standing outside as requested by the physician. They were shocked to see the king approach; they bowed as he entered the queen's rooms. The nanny who had been looking after the queen was sleeping but roused when she heard someone enter the bedroom. She nearly screamed when she realised it was the king, but he put a finger to his lips, so she understood to keep quiet. He approached his wife and could hear her softly calling Oliver's name as she slept. He kissed her gently on the cheek, and she slowly became aware of someone present beside her bed. She slowly sat up, still half asleep, yawned and stretched. Only then did she fully open her eyes and see her beloved husband. Shocked at the sight of him, she burst into tears and flung her arms around his neck as if she would never let go again.

They stayed in this embrace for what seemed an eternity. When he broke free, he said, "I have a surprise for you."

She then screamed, "Where is Oliver?" She jumped out of bed and raced to his room. Richard was right by her side. They opened the door together and there, sitting in the middle of the floor, was Oliver with his three sisters, and he was telling them of all the things that had happened on his fantastic journey. On seeing his mother, he got to his feet and ran over to her and jumped into her arms. She was crying so much, she could not speak. Between the sobs, she managed to ask how. Richard told her of the green-striped zebra and about the wish, and it was all true, thanks to Percival and his story.

Meanwhile, Dante had woken, fully expecting to be sitting on a mountain of gold, and he was. Only, it was a mountain of golden sand, in the middle of the desert, for only the pure of heart can receive the wish they desire.